RUDE BUAY

... Shatterproof

An Original Story
By
International Bestselling
Author
John A. Andrews
Creator Of:
The Rude Buay Series®

Published in the U.S.A. by
Books That Will Enhance Your Life™

A L I - Andrews Leadership International
Entertainment Division®
Jon Jef Jam Entertainment®
www.JohnAAndrews.com

Cover Design: John A. Andrews
Cover Graphic Designer: A L I
Edited by: Prof Harminder Kaur
ISBN: 978-0-9848980-1-5

RUDE BUAY

... Shatterproof

by
National Bestselling Author

John A. Andrews

Other Series

RENEGADE COPS
&
The WHODUNIT CHRONICLES

TABLE OF CONTENTS

The

RUDE BUAY

Series

Vol. III

"*The things I've been through give me fortitude. I'm not easily broken. Not only have I seen too much but I've been through too much. Selling **out** is not **in** my character. You may hang my body tomorrow but you will never hang my character.*"

- Rude Buay

1

In a chic Cul De Sac, located in the covert hills of Northern Shanghai, smoke, debris, fire, and ashes continue to rise from what's left of the sweltering *Torture House*.

Less than 24 hours ago, this domicile had housed some high profile hostages, four of the most efficient agents the world has ever seen. Fighters against narcotics, these adept drug enforcement agents who hailed from the U.S. and Jamaica have been tortured immensely by the invincible *Dragon Drug Cartel*. A descendant of a former special drug enforcement agent, HEIDI HUDSON: she's Caucasian in her late twenties. Hudson steps off the plane in Miami. Jamaican born, MILDRED SIMMS, in her late twenties. She is a drop-dead gorgeous, sophisticated African American beauty, every man's heart's desire and employed by the Ministry of Tourism in Jamaica. WALTER BANKS, a Jamaican born African American in his late fifties, with salt and pepper hair, and a veteran D.E.A. who served for many years in Colombia. The Commissioner of Police in Jamaica, RICHARD BAPTISTE, a tall, slim, kingly man in his forties.

These agents miraculously and cleverly not only made their escape before two *femme Fatales* of the *Dragon Drug Cartel* returned to kill them but were also instrumental in setting the house on fire. Agents Heidi Hudson and Mildred Simms were the ones who pulled the detonating gun triggers which set this *Torture House* ablaze, sending fumes of *Ganja* and mahogany wood into the universe as soon as those two women entered through the garage.

Later that day, fire trucks with idle engines and flashing lights continue to pour water on the remains of the burning building. While they dowse a room filled with sacks of weed: suddenly as if by a stroke of luck, an enthusiastic Chinese fireman notices some movements nearby in the large outdoor swimming pool.

The pool is partially covered with fallen burnt roofing and mahogany scaffolds, some of which are still falling into the body of water and extinguishing in the process.

In haste, multiple firefighters extend a ladder into the pool between the scaffolds while concentrating the water hose in that vicinity.

Two exhausted women accept the invitation of the aluminum ladder and begin climbing out in what's left of their street clothes amidst the burning inferno.

First on the ladder is DENISE GOMEZ. Denise is an Asian, trophy woman, in her late twenties. Her engagement ring, still touching her wedding band, is to be greatly desired by any woman. The blinding rock speaks for itself, despite her partially covered, with ash, appearance. The first firefighter rescues her. This agile fireman grabs her and escorts her to the sidewalk. They're a team of firefighters emerge and proceeds to pump water out of Denise Gomez's lungs.

Another agile firefighter quickly grabs the ascending *WWE* type SHELLY HALL and also pulls her swiftly to safety before the roof of the building caves in on top of the pool. Shelly Hall, partially covered with ash is a tall Caucasian woman in her 30s. Soon she is lying on the sidewalk. With the aid of mouth to mouth resuscitation performed by a firefighter, water pours out of her mouth and nostrils like a spurt as she coughs up some more intermittently.

Soon thereafter, both rescued *femme Fatales* are placed on separate gurneys and rushed into idling ambulances. The ambulances depart speedily while the fire trucks continue to dowse water on the smoky remains of the almost diminished *Torture House*.

MEANWHILE, IN A NOT TOO DISTANT Shanghai village, a white car cruises down the street. Inside, the driver MILES TATE navigates while surveying through the narrow Shanghai roadsides. Tate is Caucasian in his early 30s. Next to him on the front seat is a half-closed attaché case.

Meanwhile, ALBERTO GOMEZ, drug Czar and leader of the *Dragon Drug Cartel*, is on foot going down that same street. Alberto Gomez is dressed in a tattered expensive business suit and dark tinted sun glasses. He's in mid to late 30s, of Colombian descent. Alberto Gomez is bruised and bloodied over most of his body. It is evident he's been involved in a big fight or scuffle. Miles Tate stops the car and pulls over to the curb. He puts the attaché case on the rear seat and opens the front passenger door to accommodate the drug, Czar. Alberto Gomez boards on the front seat soon as the passenger door swings open.

"Thanks! Always on time, huh?"

Says Alberto Gomez.

"Like they say in Jamaica: No Problem. No problem *mon!*"

Says Tate.

Alberto Gomez seems focused.

Tate continues,

"He almost ate your lunch, huh?"

Alberto Gomez keeping it all business, questions,

"So you finished him off, yeah?"

"One shot straight for the bull's eye. He went down and that *Wood House* subsequently caved in on him."

Tate responds.

"Nice finish to that pain in the A…!"

Says Alberto Gomez.

The two men high five each other as they wait for the stoplight to go green.

"What about the hostages?"

Asks Tate.

"Without Amanda…I'm sure Denise and Shelly Hall have them bound and ready for tomorrow's hanging."

Alberto Gomez responds:

"Our first order of business will be to affix your Dragon signature as soon as I find me some new *gear* and a local tattoo shop. We have to make you official for that group hanging."

Later, Alberto Gomez pulls up at a tattoo shop. They enter the establishment run by the Tattoo King who is extravagantly tattooed all over his body. His lavish tattoo décor states clearly: I am tattooed on hands, tattooed in heart and tattooed on the brain.

2

In Montego Bay, Jamaica, investigators, along with the news media ambitiously converge on the Ministry of Tourism building. They swarm around Mildred Simms gleaning for every bit of news regarding her escape. The Caribbean beauty has just returned to the office at the Ministry of Tourism for the first time after being kidnapped by members of the high ranking *Dragon Drug Cartel*.

While the gathering media pry the information relevant to her capture and escape from the *Torture*

House, sends shockwaves through the hearts of her coworkers, awaiting their opportunity to console Jamaica's Mildred. TV cameras keep rolling, camera lights flashing, and boom mikes extending, as eager reporters recapture this remarkable hostage recovery story. They lament on her bravery for pulling the trigger which set the *Torture House* on fire.

A few blocks away at the Police Barracks, a similar scenario unfolds: the overzealous news media glean information from ex-hostage and Jamaican Police Commissioner Richard Baptiste. Standing across from the commissioner is his wife CHRISTINE BAPTISTE. Christine, a stylist in her own right is dressed to the nines. Additionally, she glows basking in the happiness of being back in Jamaica and by the side of her ex-hostage husband, Richard.

Standing next to Christine is the Governor-General Dr. Bradford Wiley, intellectually sound and in his sixties. He beams with joy to see Richard alive and well. The two men have been responsible for making multiple important decisions for fighting the war on narcotics not only in Jamaica but in the other Caribbean Islands, Asia, the U.S as well as Mexico.

The news media continue to garner information while the TV cameras roll excessively. One Spanish reporter from a Mexican affiliate radio station steps up and begins to etch notes on a yellow pad.

At home, many Jamaicans are glued to their TV sets soaking up the news.

At the Police Barracks, a microphone extends on a boom towards The Commissioner. One reporter asks:

"How did you survive this ordeal and come out of it alive after being kidnapped by the *Dragon Drug Cartel* twice in *one* month?"

"I don't know. It was more than a miracle. I must say that it was ... thanks to Rude Buay and his awesome team or else we would be..."

"And ... where is Rude Buay now?"

Another reporter asks as the camera zooms out.

"Not sure. According to reports, he is feared dead. After the building; in which he single-handedly eliminated several members of the *Dragon Drug Cartel* including Johnny *Too Bad*; collapsed on top of him. How would you categorize the presumed dead, agent Rude Buay?"

Asks the reporter.

"We owe a sincere debt of gratitude to agent Rude Buay. He wanted to create a better world for all. We were happy to be part of his mission."

Says Richard.

Before another reporter could quiz the Commissioner, two double-breasted jacket attired police officers escort him and his wife out of the room, and inside a waiting limousine. Microphones attached to booms are still against the limousine's window. The vehicle drives off leaving them hanging.

MEANWHILE, IN KINGSTON the capital city of Jamaica, drug lord MARCUS RANKS, wearing his dreadlocks hairstyle is on a tirade. Ranks an ally to the *Dragon Drug Cartel* has ordered his men to block off all streets east, west, north and south of Kingston. The Jamaican Drug Lord vowed that he would avenge the U.S., not only for extraditing Johnny *Too Bad* to America but for setting *pigs* on Johnny like a pack of dogs to snuff him out.

With water dowsed on the *Tivoli Gardens* riot, the extradition of Johnny *Too Bad* and, the Drug Lord's death, the Jamaican Law Enforcement had lapsed back into their comfort zone regarding *TG*.

Ranks, on the other hand, was planning a major comeback for the *Dragons* in *TG*, moving their new drug methamphetamine in large quantities into West Kingston. Therefore, Ranks ordered those streets heading into Kingston to be blocked off. If the police were to ever join forces and enter into *Tivoli Gardens* they would be slowed down, robbed of their weapons and then beaten to death.

The Jamaican Police Department, somewhat shorthanded at this point had to cool it somewhat when it comes to apprehending drug smugglers in *Tivoli Gardens*.

3

lberto Gomez and Miles Tate are still at the upscale Shanghai tattoo shop. Alberto admires as the petite, in stature, attendant affixes the signature of the dragons behind Tate's right ear. Miles Tate is elated as he now sports the signature of the Dragon Cartel. Alberto Gomez, now neatly attired looks clean again except for multiple facial bruises. He is always the businessman; suave and debonair, sporting his dark sunglasses. He is focused like a man on a mission.

"So where would I be stationed, Vermont or Vancouver?"

Asks Miles Tate.

Alberto Gomez's cell phone rings in the meantime, he gets it.

"*Papi...!*"

Exclaims Denise Gomez.

Denise is lying on a Shanghai hospital bed, sadly affected by second-degree burns over most of her body as a result of the *Torture House* fire. Across from her is her partner in crime Shelly Hall. With multiple burns to her body. Shelly Hall is in the same uncomfortable condition. Overwhelmed in pain, the veteran *drug lady* tries masking it. Denise Gomez is *dying to report*.

Sensing the somber tone in Denise's voice, Alberto Gomez questions,

"Why? Where are you, at the *Torture House*, planning those hangings for tomorrow?"

"No, we are at the hospital and badly burned up. The *Torture House* burned down last night. However, thanks to the swimming pool, Shelly Hall and I are still alive but badly burned up, Al."

"You got to be kidding! The Hatchback caught on fire? What happened to the ... hostages?"

Asks Alberto Gomez.

"Too Bad! When we arrived from the *Wood House*, several bullets fired out and the building exploded in flames. They got away. All four of them! Those ...

bastards escaped. It seems like it was a collaborative effort. Don't know how they pulled that one-off. Where is Rude Buay? Did you get him?"
Denise asks.
"Escaped huh? They may run but they cannot hide. They are such a minority in this city. They ought to know that. Those agents won't have a ... chance. When we catch them we will hang their ... high!" In regards to Rude Buay, we finished him off at the *Wood House*. States Alberto Gomez.
Tate eavesdrops and reacts negatively to the survival story of the hostages. He can't wrap his mind around it. Tate had envisioned joining the *Dragon Cartel* with a major advantage over its opposition - the D.E.A. and its allies. This would be his first big celebration after deflecting back in Shanghai. He so wanted to witness the hanging of agents Mildred Simms, Walter Banks, Heidi Hudson, and the Jamaican Police Commissioner Richard Baptiste. Being disappointed is an understatement.
"We are heading to the hospital ... We'll be there soon." Alberto Gomez says.
The two men look at each other in total disbelief. They reluctantly digest this latest breaking news from Denise and Shelly Hall. Distasteful as it has been, finally, Tate is the first one to speak:
"How the heck did they get out of there alive? It's like a miracle! I mean Denise and Shelly Hall. Are they half

fish, half-human? Sounds like *Déjà vu* to me. Are they mermaids?"

"They met in swim school. They handle water situations well."

Says Alberto Gomez.

"No wonder, they could have *boiled* in that swimming pool."

Says Tate.

"Who knows what condition they are in? It could be more serious than they are claiming..."

The car with the two Drug Lords on board pulls up at the hospital ER entrance and comes to a halt. Tate puts the car in park. Tate and Alberto Gomez step out and hurriedly enter the hospital compound like men on a mission.

4

Meanwhile at the hospital, after looking at their grossly burnt bodies, Alberto Gomez, Miles Tate, Denise Gomez, and Shelly Hall embark upon laying plans for a massive comeback. They envision capturing all the DEA agents and hanging them one by one from the gallows. Additionally, they also discuss plans of setting up the *Dragon Drug Cartel* headquarters in the sister-cities of Nogales in Mexico and Arizona. This would mean, however, truncating themselves from Colombia after 5 years of narcotics operation on its soil.

About 60 miles south of Tucson lie the sister-cities that share that same name - Nogales. One is in Arizona, the other in Old Mexico. Many years ago, groves of walnut trees covered the mountain pass that bridged the two, leading to the name Nogales, derived from the Spanish word for dark walnuts. Today, not only do many Americans cross the border into Nogales to acquire less costly medical care and over the counter drugs, but drug smugglers experience much ease trafficking narcotics from the Mexican border city across to the American side. The *Dragon Drug Cartel* by now was beginning to feel the need not only to capitalize but to dominate in Mexico as well. Even so, they had to move swiftly as other drug cartels also wanted to take advantage of this narcotics trafficking accessibility.

Alberto Gomez pulled out the stops as he addresses his team at the hospital double room briefing:

"Tate, as was requested by David Lee, you will be set up at Vermont, in the U.S. Canadian Border. Shelly Hall, when you return to active duty will monitor those operations.

Denise and I will handle the Nogales Border between Mexico and Arizona until we can find a competent replacement. Our priority will be to expand trade between Mexico and California as well as Mexico and Arizona. This new venture is going to be very challenging, as we will not only have to deal with other D.E.A. agents but competing cartels as well."

Alberto Gomez continues,

"I have already contacted Johnny *Too Bad*'s protégé Marcus Ranks. He will head up the Tivoli Garden operation, thus putting it back on the map. We cannot leave Jamaica out of the mix. It is still our breadbasket our bread and butter. We miss Johnny *Too Bad* but we have to move on, that is the trend of this business."

SAMMY CHIN an ally of David Lee will head up China along with the rest of Asia.

GRACE McCLOUD will replace Amanda Kingsley and monitor our Miami operations. SALVADOR will be ready to start shipping soon. We may need him temporarily in Bogotá at this point."

"I thought Sal was in…"

Questions Miles Tate.

"I have a connection with some of the authorities over there at the Shanghai prison. We stand a very good chance of getting him out of there. You are in good hands with us, Tate."

Responds Alberto Gomez.

"We could be back in the trade in less than two weeks. Denise's and Shelly's wounds would heal soon and we will be back in business for good."

"I can't wait to get out of here guys, can't wait to join you."

Chimes Shelly Hall.

"You and me both of us,"
Adds Denise Gomez.
Before that brief emergency meeting of the drug-smuggling-minds is about to be adjourned, a piece of late-breaking news; far too coincidentally close to their train of thought; from the *ABC News* channel, catches their attention. They all glue in on to the two small TV sets inside the double hospital room:

"Five people found burned beyond recognition in an abandoned SUV in an area of Arizona frequented by smugglers were likely the victims of one of the same drug cartels that have ravaged parts of Mexico with their rampant violence, the local sheriff said today.

A border patrol agent noticed a white Ford Expedition stopping around 4:30 a.m. Saturday in Vekol Valley, a desert area that's a well-known smuggling corridor for drugs and illegal immigrants from Mexico. Suspecting the car stopped to pick up drugs, the agent tried to make contact with the vehicle, but the vehicle fled.

When the sun came up, the agent noticed car tracks leading off the road and followed them for a couple of miles into the desert. The agent found a smoldering vehicle and called for back-up. When other agents arrived, they used fire extinguishers to put out the fire and found five charred bodies inside the car, say the police.

"This is pretty significant," Pinal County Sheriff Paul Babeu said. "Given all these indicators, you don't have to be a homicide detective to add up all the information."

One victim was found in the sedan's rear passenger seat and four others in the back cargo compartment, their bodies burned beyond recognition.

Investigators have not yet determined whether the bodies were bound, the sheriff said.

Babeu told ABC News that it's likely others fled the scene.

"There wasn't anyone in the front driver's seat or the front passenger's seat and the position of the bodies lead us to believe that it's most likely that other people were aboard it," Babeu said.

Babeu said the deaths are being investigated as homicides.

"The vehicle was stopped in an open area. It did not crash into something. Clearly whoever murdered these people did it intentionally," he said. "They brought them there either alive or dead and torched the vehicle to conceal the evidence."

Babeu said the incident is likely a case of drug cartel violence.

"This is more than likely connected to drug smuggling," he said. "It's most likely not human smuggling because most of the time if the illegal person is no longer of use or too slow for the rest of the group, they're left to fend for themselves or die. We don't see many cases where illegal people are killed. They're usually only killed if they put up a fight as they're being robbed.

"This is more likely either punishment on criminals who tried to steal from the cartels or some competing interest in a criminal element."

Babeu said investigators will try to determine whether the victims were dead before the fire was started or whether they were alive when the SUV was set ablaze.

The Vekol Valley is located 70 miles north of the U.S.-Mexican border. Babeu called the area a "hotbed for human and drug smuggling."

The federal government put up 15 billboards that read: "Danger Warning, Travel Not Recommended, Drug Smuggling, Active and Armed Gunmen" in the area along Interstate 8.

Last year, the Vekol Valley was the site of the largest drug bust in the history of Arizona.

Seventy-six members of the Sinaloa cartel were arrested in the bust, known as Operation Pipeline Express. The suspects had 108 weapons, including scoped rifles, AK47s and two weapons from the U.S. government's Fast & Furious program.

The controversial program, run by the Bureau of Alcohol, Tobacco, Firearms, and Explosives, was designed to track guns bought in the United States by straw men and delivered to drug cartels in Mexico, in an attempt to catch the cartel higher-ups. Begun in 2009, it was shut down after the December 2010 murder of U.S. Border Patrol agent Brian Terry, who was killed with a weapon sold through the program.

Babeu said, the fact that the Fast & Furious guns were found in the possession of the Sinaloa cartel members, is a sign that the program is "criminal."

"We will be back with more in a minute."

The attending nurse walks in and signals five more minutes. She then departs.

Tate looks across at Alberto Gomez, so do Denise and Shelly Hall as they reminisce on this previous Associated Press report:

Ten suspected gangsters were killed Thursday morning during a running gun-battle in the Mexican border town of Nogales, just one week after the U.S. State Department warned of growing violence among narcotics rings.

Mexican media said Sonoran justice officials confirmed the number dead and reported that several police officers were injured by shrapnel when fleeing suspects tossed grenades at them. No law enforcement agents were reported dead.

The events in Nogales were part of a bloody day along the nearly 2,000-mile Mexican border, where 21 people died in 24 hours of violence involving drug traffickers and other criminal syndicates.

In Ciudad Juarez, along with the Texas reporter, the Associated Press reported four men were shot dead in front of a crowd at an amusement park and a toddler died when the car he was in crashed during a gun-battle. Also, a businessman was murdered after leading a protest against violence.

This is a very, very dangerous time to be a drug agent, said Beth Kempshall, special agent in charge of the Drug Enforcement Administration in Phoenix. The stakes are greater right here in Arizona than I've ever seen them.

Kempshall said the situation in Nogales was still unfolding Wednesday afternoon, and information was sketchy. The number of bodies, it was still in chaos, she noted. It wasn't a good situation down there.

The Tucson Citizen reported that shootings began around 6 a.m. as police stopped a pair of vehicles containing suspected gangsters. It was not immediately clear whether that incident was preceded by fighting between narcotics groups or something else. Officers pursued the suspects along major Nogales streets, with at least two battles occurring a few miles from the border.

Four suspects reportedly died after officers shot out a vehicle's tires, causing it to crash. Others were killed by gunfire. Three civilians also suffered minor injuries during the fighting, according to the Citizen.

Last week, D.E.A. officials said violence in Sonora is growing because outside narcotics organizations are challenging the so-called Sinaloa cartel, which for years claimed dominion over smuggling routes into Arizona. Kempshall said a crackdown by the Mexican government and increased pressure by U.S. agents had added friction: They're fighting over the routes into the United States, and over control of the border area.

Brian Levin, a spokesman for Customs and Border Protection, said U.S. entry ports are always prepared for violence, so no additional security measures are in place.

The State Department alert said Nogales is among several border cities that have recently experienced public shootouts during daily hours. Conflicts involving heavily armed gangsters claimed about 3,000 lives in Mexico this year. In September, there were at least five public gun-battles, including the murder of a man next to a school. Last week, gunmen fired hundreds of rounds into the home of a Nogales reporter, who was not injured.

On Wednesday in Ciudad Juarez, four men were shot inside an amusement park where teenagers were riding bikes through obstacle courses, skating, and rappelling.

Elsewhere in the city, a used car salesman was shot to death while driving down the main boulevard hours after leading hundreds of other business owners in a protest against kidnappings and extortion. The demonstrators had threatened to close their businesses or stop paying taxes because so many were being targeted by extortionists demanding up to $500 a week for protection against crime.

In Tijuana a 1-year-old boy was killed, when the car he was riding in crashed, as the driver tried to flee a gunfight late Wednesday between the police and three armed men, officials in the state prosecutor's office said. The toddler had been sitting in his mother's lap.

"There is no more Rude Buay to interfere and whoever Michael Ortiz puts in his place is not ready for such a force as us. Neither is the Sinaloa Cartel. The bozo heading it up doesn't even know his left hand from his right."

Miles Tate proclaims.

"As for Rude Buay's replacement, there is no one to put in Rude Buay's place as far as I know. Heidi Hudson is not ready for such a task. He was her strength, a shoulder she leaned on. Those Jamaican agents are nothing, very incompetent. Michael Ortiz would not take us on by himself. I doubt he would use them."

Adds Denise Gomez.

The nurse returns to the room. They abruptly adjourn the meeting. Alberto Gomez kisses Denise on her lips. He then quickly departs with ex-agent and now ally, Miles Tate.

5

Methamphetamine, cocaine, heroin along with other narcotics pour into Nogales - Arizona, El Paso, San Diego, Canada, Miami, China and the Jamaican cities of Tivoli Gardens, Kingston and Port Antonio - originated from Nogales, Mexico. Truckers carefully unload their cargo in these major drug smuggling cities. The dealers arrive and pick up the drugs in their high-end automobiles. They distribute them to buyers at parks, grocery stores, clubs, parking garages, yachts, and airplane hangars. While some deliver at more secret locations like back alleys and business offices.

Getting high on the streets from cocaine, meth, and other drugs have become the thing to do as if drugs have been legalized. You could walk down most any street and buy narcotics just like you would candy or bottled water. For so many drug addicts their new long-lasting high comes from the drug Methamphetamine.

On the street; this brain and body killer drug Methamphetamine or Meth; is more commonly sold under names as crank, speed, crystal or ice. This whitish or pale yellow crystal-like powder is normally chewed, ingested, injected, snorted or sometimes smoked.

Methamphetamine, sold in large quantities, is a powerfully intense stimulant that creates a euphoric and energetic feeling. It releases high levels of the neurotransmitter dopamine, which stimulates brain cells, enhancing mood and body movement.

While cocaine high lasts about 15-20 minutes, a meth high lasts 2-14 hours. The *Dragon Drug Cartel* uses this opportune sales pitch to push Meth like none other.

Drug users and pushers alike trading on the streets seems to have no respect for law enforcement. The plea of most drug users is: "legalize drugs so the price would drop." Many even say: "Legalize drugs so people can have easy access without interference from the police."

On the other hand, most Jamaican law enforcement authorities have seen enough living through the *Tivoli Gardens* riots and with the streets in Kingston being blocked off recently. They wouldn't fall for that legalization phenomenon. In Jamaica, the police beef up their operation and arrest many narcotics offenders including several young adult drug smugglers.

IN THE INTERIM; WHILE DENISE GOMEZ AND SHELLY HALL recuperate from their injuries; profits from Methamphetamine around the globe, soar at an amazing pace. Unfortunately, though, these profits do not flow to the *Dragon Drug Cartel*; they had previously focused their efforts on the profits from the drug cocaine in Colombia.

Alberto Gomez realizes that despite all of their worthy plans and past successes, they have been only been playing from the periphery of the game. Miles Tate and Gomez concentrate on playing "catching up" to the *Sinaloa Drug Cartel*, who outshone them in every way possible.

Hence Gomez decides to revert to the young, the innocent, and the gadded to move meth expediently from Mexico across the U.S. borders, to catch up with his competitors.

MEANWHILE, ACROSS THE U.S./MEXICAN El Paso border, a stand-off ensues as U.S. Border Patrol Officers confront and seize over 500 pounds of Methamphetamine, a street value of over $20,000,000.00 (20 million dollars) in Miami.

Several smugglers transporting the substance in cars were detained and arrested as they tried to illegally transport them across and into the U.S. Even as these smugglers were placed in handcuffs by U.S. border patrols, the *Dragon Drug Cartel* sent in over 2 dozen pre-teenagers, recently trained at a firing range to combat the attacks made by the border patrols on those smugglers.

In the interim, while the El Paso border patrols were busily conducting their investigation of the smugglers, those same over 2 dozen kids ages 11-12 stormed through the Mexican city of Nogales and across the U.S. border into the Arizonian city of Nogales, demanding a release of the smugglers and their seized narcotics.

Armed with AK47s they confronted the investigation focused border officers, shooting and killing many. It was said that the El Paso border patrols did not even the score. Instead of retaliating those officers choose not to return fire because they realized that they were dealing with a bunch of minors or what some may call *Generation K2-10.*

By the time those border patrol officers reverted to tear gas to restrain the kids, many of them were already gunned down by the antagonistic pre-teenagers.

The arrested smugglers were then released by the efforts of the minors who stormed into the border's detention center. Using keys found at fallen border patrols desks they unlocked the handcuffs of the detained and set them free.

Upon their release, the smugglers continued on their trafficking routes throughout the U.S., as well as Canada.

After the vicious shoot-out; which left many border officers dead; the kids were reinforced with other minors as back-ups penetrating the Mexican city of Nogales in SUVs, spraying bullets like rain from the machine and sub-machine guns.

It wasn't until their bullets ran out that the still alive officers stationed at the border and those who were rushed in to defend as well, were, able to catch up with many of these pre-teenagers trying to flee back into Mexico. At the end of this standoff between the minors and border patrols, over one dozen minors were arrested.

The others took flight and fled into the hills of the Mexican desert. For days, later on, the Mexican Police combed through the desert equipped with tear gas in search of those remaining kid shooters. Days and days of searching, unfortunately, produced negative results as the police returned empty-handed.

The kids, on the other hand, had returned safely to the base camp of the *Dragons* in Southern Nogales and sought refuge. There, they continued their combat training under the auspices of Drug Czar Alberto Gomez, leader of the infamous *Dragon Drug Cartel*.

Greg Bascombe an African Jamaican in his mid-40s is the dad of two daughters. Greg lives in Jamaica with his family. His wife BRENDA BASCOMBE is Caucasian and in her late 30s. Together the Bascombe family is raising their twin teenage daughters, GLENDA and THELMA.

Greg is one of Jamaica's finest at the Port Antonio Police Department. His tenure in law enforcement dates back almost a decade. He is also a leader in his church, revered by the young and old alike. Greg is the youth pastor as well as the church treasurer. His wife Brenda is a church elder who sits on the church board and is part of every major decision that the organization makes.

At fourteen the girls are straight "A" students. Thelma wants to become a doctor and Glenda a missionary. Additionally, they are the talk of their church and the community. They excel in just about everything they touch. Putting it subtly, the girls are evolving into Port Antonio's Model Citizens.

Lately, though, Greg has diverted into a slump. His ways are uncanny. Not only has he been missing important appointments, but he has been hanging out with his high school buddies at regular freebasing and meth consumption sessions.

Brenda, noticing Greg's unaccountability suggests that they start attending counseling with their senior pastor Douglas Cambridge. Greg has a big ego and refuses, not wanting to submit his ego to another man. At church, although the Bascombe's put on a façade of a tight-knit family with all of their ducks in a row, at home the family is falling apart at the seams.

One Sunday afternoon after church, Greg leaves his car at home and asks one of his high school buddies to pick him up. Together they drive to a house where three of their other ex-school mates join them for a freebasing session.

In the interim, Glenda visits her dad's car parked on the street. She rummages through the car. In the glove compartment, she discovers not only almost one gram of cocaine but methamphetamine, along with freebasing utensils. She is ecstatic and indulges.

Narcotics usage has been an evolving habit for young Glenda. For several weeks she has been sneaking into her dad's car every time he's away and subsequently acquiring her fix. Additionally, some of her peers had on several occasions brought meth to school. To say the least, the young teen has gradually become an addict and would often join her classmates for their regular get-high sessions during lunch breaks. Then they would return to class flying on cloud nine.

This time around, her high gives her the cravings for more and more methamphetamine. She finds herself licking the foil paper clean of all residues with her tongue not fearing if her dad would realize his product has been tampered with.

Gradually and oblivious to Glenda, the meth intake had been wearing on her brain and body over time, causing both to deteriorate.

Later, Glenda walks the streets solo in high spirits. She enters the ramp and onto the major highway. Several vehicles are traveling at high speed. The driver of the oncoming eighteen-wheeler tractor trailer sees her staggering across the road. He applies brakes. Even so,

RUDE BUAY VOL. III

unable to stop the trailer he runs her over, crushing her under the vehicle's wheels.

Other vehicles crash into the trailer creating a multiple-vehicle collision. Many injuries occur. Lives are lost in this multiple-vehicle accident including the driver of the trailer. As the vehicle slams into the median upon impact, the driver is tossed from inside the truck and onto the street. It is a massive automobile pile-up with multiple vehicles colliding and forming a heap.

There's pandemonium in the chicest community of Port Antonio as neighbors rush to the scene. Brenda and Thelma making dinner get the sad news and hurry to the scene on foot and in tears.

In the meantime Greg, bathed in remorse; after hearing the sad news; gets dropped off at the house in a taxi. His colleagues, so high on meth were unable to drive him home.

Greg gets to his car and decides to drive to the scene. He notices the foil paper on the seat and clues in on the scenario: His narcotics which he had confiscated during a recent drug bust and which had intentionally not been transferred to the station had been tampered with by his daughter. He races to the scene of the accident still under the influence.

Upon arriving at the scene, and noticing the mayhem, Greg Bascombe armed on his off day reaches inside his gun holster. He removes his gun and shoots himself in the head.

The sound of the gunshot alerts those at the scene including his wife and daughter, along with his neighbors and other attending police officers.

It is too much not only for his family but for the small community of chic Port Antonio to unravel on that Sunday afternoon. There are wailing and lamentation of the community. Brenda and Thelma are discombobulated. Many cries go out on their behalf. Their church members show up in droves providing comfort during the moments of double grief.

7

Through the upscale Port Antonio community, traffic is at a standstill as funeral-goers by the hundreds proceed to the cemetery. Some mourners, traveling in buses, cars, on motorbikes and others on foot are still saddened with the shock of the double narcotics-related suicide.

Leading the procession is a motorcade of Jamaican police officers displaying the Green, Black, and Gold, on motorbikes, followed in tow by two wreath covered hearses. Spectators, sitting on their porches, verandas, and patios are bathed in tears as the procession passes the village. Motorists yield and give way to the saddened procession in a tear- shedding homage to the dead.

Meanwhile, the regretful multicultural, multiethnic, multiage procession with songs of praise wipe their crying eyes as they travel along the streets of Port Antonio.

Even while the news media in Jamaica are lashing out against the Mexicans for infiltrating their country with Methamphetamine, multiple kilos of coke and other drugs rapidly continue to contaminate the Jamaican community. Getting high has radically become the "thing" to do. Not doing it says that you are square or have a serious problem with the most important person – YOURSELF.

While some maintain the stance that if there are no customers to buy drugs, no drugs would get sold. Something no drug dealer wants to hear knowing fully that the buck stops with the client.

The funeral procession arrives at the cemetery. Glenda Ann Marie Bascombe is laid to rest. While the grave diggers fill that grave with soil, the minister prepares for the burial service of her dad Police Officer Greg Patrick Bascombe, the cousin of agent Randy Bascombe, adjacent and a few feet away.

The black, green and gold Jamaican flag covering his casket is removed by a fellow Jamaican police officer. His casket is then lowered into the grave.

It is a dual solemn occasion as more tears are shed by mourners. Glenn's wife Brenda and daughter Thelma standing at the head of the gravesite breakdown once again and are comforted by a group of consoling women.

At the end of the ceremony, the gravediggers fill this other grave also with soil as the mourners amble away from what will go down in history as the most tragic twin burial in Jamaica.

8

black BMW pulls up outside a house in MO'
Bay. TAMARA ROSS, the stunningly eye-
catching-mid to late twenty-year-old beauty
steps out. She proceeds to retrieve her keys to unlock
the house door. Her cell-phone rings at the same time.
She answers it. The call creates a sense of urgency as
she heads back to the car and takes off speedily. The
automobile screeches around the bend in the road as
Dr. Ross puts the pedal to the metal.

From many miles away the sound of a speeding ambulance siren echoes. Meanwhile, a Chinese Private Jet makes its presence felt as it takes off to the skies from MO' Bay airport. Earlier a passenger on a gurney was seen deplaning from that aircraft.

The early morning traffic is now bumper to bumper as the BMW navigates its way through the huge traffic gridlock.

Suddenly, the driver of a tailgating minivan loses focus and rear-ends the BMW. This mayhem brings traffic to a standstill; as the drivers of both vehicles involved are now caught up in accessing the damage done to their vehicles. After the settlement with the exchange of information the standstill traffic proceeds. Tamara continues her journey.

Dr. Tamara Ross' car pulls into the parking lot of MO' Bay Hospital's, ER entrance. She races to the emergency room. The nurse on duty says to her, "He's in room #26!"

Dr. Ross rushes upstairs to that room. The patient lying in bed is no stranger to her, but this is the first time that she has been entrusted with the responsibility of possibly doctoring him back to health.

Agent RANDY BASCOMBE better is known as *RUDE BUAY* aka "Rude Boy" is of Jamaican descent. He opens his eyes and smiles at Dr. Ross. Rude Buay, in his early forties, is adorned with a scorpion tattooed to his bald head, with its fangs upstaging his forehead, and a tail extending towards his right earlobe. He is also badly bruised and battered. Dr. Ross returns the smile.

"How are you felling agent?"

She asks coyly.

"How soon can you get me out of here?"

Rude Buay asks.

"I am going to have to diagnose your condition first before I can determine the length of your recovery. From what I can tell: you seem to have been badly hurt. I don't know how you survived. In so far as I know, there isn't a quick-fix recovery method in medicine, for a building falling on someone. I saw that collapsed building. You got out of there alive, that's a miracle in itself!"

Rude Buay smiles again.

"So how soon?"

Asks Rude Buay.

Dr. Ross continues.

"Why didn't you get fixed up in Shanghai or the United States? They can rush the healing process. Are you here for treatment or some TLC?"

"I picked Jamaica because of your expertise... I wouldn't trust anyone with putting me back together again."

Tamara is flattered. She leans in and kisses Rude Buay on the cheek.

"Don't worry. I'll get you out of here in record time."

She assures Rude Buay.

Tamara checks the chart and begins attaching I-vies to the agent's body. As Rude Buay begins to fall asleep, she administers to his many wounds.

At the Emergency Room, a patient is wheeled in suffering from gunshot wounds. Dr. Tamara Ross gets the call. She concludes the dressing of Rude Buay's wounds and heads to the E.R.

FLASHBACK:

At the *Wood House*, Rude Buay finally wakes up. He rolls over and realizes that he's been trapped beneath the rubble. He immediately embarks on setting himself free. It is a tedious task as multiple wood timbers press their weight against his body. He twists and turns continuously.

Finally, Rude Buay manages to squeeze his way out of the rubble. He sees a lighted area and crawls to it. He hears a neighing sound and reflects his first encounter with the horseback at *The Lodge*. To Rude Buay's surprise, the horse is also trying to remove objects with its mouth to gain access to the interior of the collapsed building where he is trapped. It finally gains access.

Rude Buay, in pain, climbs upon its back and rides across the street. Two Chinese Policemen guarding the structure notice him drenched in blood and rush to his aid.

Later, upon Rude Buay's request, they put him on a private jet bound for Jamaica.

BACK TO PRESENT:

Dr. Ross re-opens the door to Rude Buay's room. She notices he is still fast asleep. The doctor smiles, closes the door and departs.

9

L ater, at MO Bay Hospital, agent Rude Buay sits up in bed gleaning through the newspaper *Jamaican Gleaner*. The headlines read: **Jamaican Police Officer Glen Patrick Bascombe and Teen Daughter Commit Meth Related Suicides In Port Antonio.** Rude Buay gives the page heading multiple second looks. He knows Glen. Not only are they related cousins, but they also went to High School together. As he reads the front page news horrified, Rude Buay can't help reflecting on the death of his brother Clifford, over a decade ago in a drug-related incident outside their tenement yard in Jamaica. He can still see his mother holding his blood-drenched brother in her arms before the Jamaican police conducting their investigation and him standing next to her along with his godmother Maude Davis.

Rude Buay tosses the newspaper aside and focuses on the I-vies still attached to his body as he tries to roll onto his side but feels trapped. Suddenly, the screen opens and Dr. Tamara Ross enters. Looking at Rude Buay she says,

"How was your rest?"

"I guess my thoughts were so centered on getting out of here, I don't recall resting except that it was a mixture of dreams and nightmares."

Says Rude Buay.

"You've got to follow the doctor's orders. Rest is a must if you want a speedy recovery, my dear."

Tamara encourages.

She continues,

"So what was the dream?"

"I had a dream about you but then woke up and began reading the front page of the *Jamaican Gleaner*. There, unfortunately, I learned about my cousin and his daughter's drug-related suicide."

"Which copy was that?"

Asks Tamara.

Tamara picks up the paper and stares at the headlines.

"No wonder, and you missed his funeral. I had no idea you all were related."

"Good guy, bad situation."

"Yep. I am glad that you survived."

She comments as she puts down the newspaper. As she cleans and dresses Rude Buays' wounds she probes,

"The dream? ... and about me?"

Asks Tamara,

"I'll save that for when I can stand on my own two feet. "

Says Rude Buay,

"Why do men always want to make women wait?

Asks Tamara,

"Why? Because ... you all do the same thing to us."

Says Rude Buay.

"I am not sure that is medically correct."

Responds Dr. Ross.

"I want to let you know that as your physician, my duty is two-fold. I still don't trust any nurse taking care of you."

Adds Tamara Ross.

Rude Buay admires Tamara as she unfolds her thoughts.

"I don't blame you, after that previous dilemma with the nurse and Axel James several months ago at the Port Antonio hospital; one never knows who is connected."

Tamara reattaches the life support to Rude Buay and reaches inside her purse. She removes her cell phone and shows Rude Buay pictures of Jamaican Policemen guarding the corridor as well as the checkpoint at the hospital's entrance.

She then retrieves a semi-automatic gun from her larger purse and hands it to Rude Buay.

He checks the gun and sees that it is silencer attached as well as fully loaded. He puts it carefully underneath his pillow.

Dr. Ross answers her cellular pager. She has to go. She blows Rude Buay a kiss and departs.

10

Tamara ambles through the parking lot. She gets inside her car and drives up to the hospital's security checkpoint. There she is stopped, although still attired with the stethoscope around her neck; she is detained, her car is also searched thoroughly by two Jamaican Police Officers. She is later given the *green-light*. Tamara views the situation as just a routine check and continues on her way unaffected. Several miles up the road, she notices something through her rearview mirror and senses being followed. This vehicle has been tailing her BMW for more than a mile. She speeds up. Her perpetrator does vice versa. She accesses her car phone and immediately dials 911. A rookie officer picks up the call at Montego Bay Police Station.

Tamara reports the fact of the matter to the officer, who asks:

"What is your location, Miss Ross?"

"Heading west on Overlook Way,"

She responds.

"What is the make and model of the vehicle trailing you?"

Asks the still wet behind his ears police officer.

"It's a black SUV. No front license tags."

Responds Dr. Ross.

"What does the driver look like?"

Asks the officer.

"It looks like two men wearing dark sunglasses and dark suits."

Dr. Ross responds.

"Where are you now?"

The officer asks.

"At the peak of Hilltop Road, I pulled off from the regular route going to my house and they are still in pursuit. You need to send in a response team right away!"

Explains Dr. Ross.

"Miss Ross ..."

Responds the officer.

Dr. Ross interrupts,

"Why... all of these questions? Don't you get it that I am being followed for several miles by a pursuer who will not let up?"

A female officer interrupts and intercepts the conversation.

"Miss Ross, Don't panic, drive normally. We are on our way. That is a lonely stretch of road. However, there is a shopping center two miles up the road you may want to pull into that busy mall. We will be there soon."

Dr. Ross speeds up and sees the huge shopping mall beckoning in the distance. Before she could make that exit to the mall, the trailing SUV speeds up, passes and appears in front of her BMW.

Dr. Ross stops her car and attempts to make a U-Turn. Before she could position her car for that getaway turn, the two armed men jump out and surround her vehicle. The doctor makes sure her doors are locked. One of the men breaks the driver's window using a crowbar.

The Doctor yells for help. Her cries are not heard by anyone except the two men as she is still a great distance away from that mall.

The two men drag her out of the car. They tape up her mouth. They bind her with ropes and throw her in the back of their SUV and re-board their vehicle. The speeding SUV departs from the scene continuing on its recent path.

11

A Jamaican Police Officer sneaks into Rude Buay's room. The officer looks around the room. Rude Buay's eyes are closed. The officer attempts to remove the life support attached to the agent's wrist. Rude Buay opens his eyes and senses the officer's motive. Realizing that the agent is helpless and unable to defend himself the officer removes the life support attached to the monitor and reaches for the one attached to the agent's arm.

In the interim Rude Buay reaches underneath his pillow and retrieves his gun. Before the officer could bring out and engage his pistol Rude Buay shoots him in the face with the silencer-attached weapon.

Some time elapses as Rude Buay tries to make his way out of bed. The other officer realizing his partner has not returned barges inside Rude Buay's hospital room. Rude Buay hears his footsteps and sees him coming.

Rude Buay, though in pain arms himself and slumps back in the bed. He fires off a round that hits the police officer in his head. The officer topples over to the ground dead. Now two officers are lying bloodied and dead on the floor of his hospital room.

Rude Buay makes another effort to get out of there. He is not even focusing on the detached life support which hangs from the machine. Even so, it seems like he is trapped inside that room.

MEANWHILE, A NURSE filing away papers in her office notices a stack of fresh sheets undelivered to room # 26, the same room in which Rude Buay resides. So, she checks the housekeeping records.

Additionally, she checks the records more in-depth and realizes that Dr. Tamara Ross has not reported for work in some time.

"If she did show up those bedsheets would not be sitting in that room."

Says the nurse, as she picks up the bedsheets, and heads swiftly to room # 26.

Upon entering the room, she notices a silhouette sitting on the agent's bed with a pointed gun in his hand. Not only is the gun pointed at her, she also notices the two dead bodies on the floor. The site of the blood-drenched uniformed police officers makes her quiver. Retracting the curtain she notices agent Rude Buay sitting up in bed with his gun pointed at her. She screams out.

"Help!"

She drops the bedsheets on the ground and darts out of the hospital ward and back to her office. She goes to her desk and calls in hospital security.

There is a male patient in another bed in that hospital ward with his leg propped up in a cast. He hears the cry for help. He tries moving off the bed to assist in the situation.

In the meantime, Rude Buay looks out the window then back inside the room. The distance between his room and the ground level descends many stories. In a state of panic, he grabs the blood-stained bedsheets off the floor, picks up his gun and ties it around his neck using the pillowcase.

He gets out onto the ledge of the window. Finally, he ties those sheets together like a rope and attaches one end to the window's bar. Holding on to the strung-together sheets he makes his descent.

Inside the hospital, security guards are alerted. They emerge racing to his room followed by the same nurse. The patient with the leg in cast aches as he hurts his leg in the process of getting up to assist. By this time the security guards arrive at Rude Buays' room and look through that opened window, Rude Buay has already made it to the ground level of the hospital. They race out in pursuit.

Rude Buay sprints to the morgue area. He sees a hearse parked next to the *dead house*. He tries the driver's door. It's open. The agent looks inside for the ignition keys. There are none. His bullet wound in the leg begins to bleed severely. He runs inside the morgue. There is nothing to stop the bleeding. A dead man lies on a gurney with a sheet wrapped around him. Rude Buay removes the sheet. The dead man is dressed in black trousers, a white shirt, and a bow tie. He rips the sheet and uses a portion of it to wrap around his wound. He then removes his hospital attire, throws them on the floor and rids the dead man of his clothing, He puts them on. He finally discovers a pack of bandages while getting dressed. He grabs it and returns to the hearse.

Rude Buay pulls the vehicle's hood lever. The hood pops open. He hot-wires the vehicle and makes his getaway through the back streets of the hospital and merges with the flow of the main street traffic.

Meanwhile, the security guards at the hospital return to their posts unaccomplished on their pursuit of Rude Buay.

12

Rude Buay pulls up across the street from a church. He parks the hearse and walks to the hotel up the block. He gets a hotel room. Once inside he begins to attend to his wounds using the bandage. His phone rings. It's Michael Ortiz, his boss in Miami.

"Rude Buay, how is the recuperation process?"

"My wounds are being attended to as we speak."

Says Rude Buay.

"Can you speak now?"

"Yes. I am by myself."

"Really?"

"Go ahead!"

"How soon can we expect you back in Miami?'

"Are you asking me to return to Miami or are you suggesting that I return. While I am still...?"

Rude Buay notices that his wound is bleeding more than before.

"Medical conditions here are superb. Plus we have drug-related issues here in the U.S. too, you know." Says Ortiz.

"Boss, I still have dual citizenship and always will. The drug crisis here has expanded tremendously. Methamphetamine is on the rise. I recently lost my cousin and his daughter. The *Dragons* are not letting up. We are in a situation where this country needs a lot of help to fight this war on drugs. What is the availability of agent Hudson?"

"Rude Buay, I am afraid that you've gotten in way too deep. You were only on loan from the U.S. remember? And now you are asking to have agent Hudson join you again? Since you took on this Caribbean vacation, we have lost three agents. Two of them you shot and killed yourself and one who has recently deflected."

"Boss, if you were to ask agent Hudson if she would rather be working in the Caribbean over Miami, I can bet she will say the Caribbean any day. Plus, it's ludicrous I must say, to blame me for the misdeeds of others. They were traitors…"

"Apparently you've brainwashed her enough that she will cover for you as she has always done, Rude Buay."

"If the war on narcotics is ever going to be won, at our level I would say we need the best fighters, those who would not whimper but fight to the … end. You have read it in the news: The cartels are now getting their guns from the *Fast & Furious* program. What's next?" States Rude Buay.

"I will ask her tomorrow and get back to you. But I am not going to twist her arm."

Rude Buay hangs up the phone expecting agent Hudson for sure to buy into his concept.

He continues to freshen up and administers to his wounds. That same evening a rental car company drops off a car for the agent. He picks up a pair of shoes at a nearby store and drives through the city hoping there's a chance he would run into Dr. Tamara Ross. His search for her is in vain. So the agent returns to his hotel room unaccomplished.

Rude Buay calls Chelo his Colombian counterpart to see if he could be of any assistance in tracking down Tamara's whereabouts using his spy gadgets.

13

Chelo, in his mid-30s and of Colombian descent is fiddling with his multiple spy gadgetries. He takes a break and answers the phone.

"Rude Buay! Man, it's sure good to hear from you. Sorry about that satellite failure in Shanghai. Anyway, I heard you survived according to Ortiz. How can I help you?"

"The *Dragon Drug Cartel* has possibly kidnapped Dr. Ross. She has been missing from the hospital for several days now. I need some help to track her whereabouts."

Says Rude Buay.

"You know how tough it is transmitting signals out of Jamaica. Too many ... interceptions! Plus since Miles Tate gave the 411 regarding our operation to the *Dragons*. They could clue in on our whereabouts easily. Try Walter Banks he might be able to assist better in the present circumstances."

Rude Buay hangs up that call and dials.

WALTER BANKS, the veteran agent is reading about a Mexican drug account in the *Jamaican Gleaner*. Banks is an African American man with salt and pepper hair and in his fifties.

"Good to hear from you Rude Buay. I thought the doctor was looking after you. At least that's what Mildred conveyed to us before our planned meeting with the Commissioner to honor you with a eulogy."

"Mildred always seems to know where I am. Doesn't she?"

States Rude Buay,

"The Commissioner and I had already discussed the tragedy and felt there was no way you would survive the collapse of the *Wood House*. Now that you are unbreakable like that "Six Million Dollar Man", I know it won't be long before we teamed up again." I'll see what I can come up with through my existing local connections. As you may have already learned our main satellite source has become problematic."

Says Banks.

"Let's do it sooner than later."

Says Rude Buay.

"Nothing from Chelo, huh?"

Asks Banks.

"It has become very problematic for him since they took out our Colombian satellites in Bogotá."

Says Rude Buay.

"Okay, I'll see what I can find."

Says Banks.

"I will be counting on you!"

14

Later Rude Buay is alerted by an email on his laptop. He checks it. The email is from Tamara. He is somewhat relieved.

Until he starts reading it,

It states:

Dear Rude Buay,

I hope you have stopped pursuing the Dragon Drug Cartel. It's a waste of your time. Any day now I could be hanged and fed to vultures. I miss you, Rude Buay. Thanks for the times we've shared. All the best with your recovery.

XOXO Tamara.

Sandals, MO' Bay.

Rude Buay is confused. This is not like Tamara. He ponders:

"Is that all she wrote? Was she pressured by fear tactics by the kidnappers; forcing her into writing this twisted style of email?"

These questions and other similar ones riddle his mind. While he applies a fresh bandage to his wounds and gets dressed. He takes up the gun which Tamara left him at the hospital. He looks it over. He is satisfied; the gun is still loaded minus the two used bullets. He straps the gun underneath his pullover jacket. He retrieves another gun that belonged to one of the fallen officers at the hospital and straps it around his leg underneath his trousers.

Rude Buays' phone rings. Walter Banks is on the line. Banks alerts Rude Buay that Tamara was reportedly seen at *Sandals* in Montego Bay. With that confirmation of her location, he ensures his weapons are intact. He heads out speedily and asks Banks to cover as back up. Banks agrees.

RUDE BUAY PULLS UP outside *Sandals*. This famous Hotel and restaurant are buzzing with activity. Parking attendants valet cars in rapid succession. Patrons mingle all over the compound. He moseys inside the resort with caution. As soon as he enters the lobby an armed man approaches him and sticks a gun in the back. Still, he manages to bring out the gun underneath his pullover in confrontation.

The man proceeds up through the hotel's stairway. Rude Buay follows looking for another good aim to blast the perpetrator.

Before he could make his way up the second set of stairs, a door from that floor level opens, he tries to reach for the other gun under his trousers. Another man grabs him from behind and wrestles the gun away from him. The man manages to *floor* Rude Buay. Instantly the other perpetrator runs back down the stairs. Together they drag him back outside through the exit door. They have a hard time restraining the agent who is valiantly putting up a fight. One of the men lets up and reaches inside his jacket pocket and pulls out a syringe. He sticks a needle in his arm and injects fluid into that arm.

Unknown to Rude Buay the two men were also involved in the authoring of the email sent by Tamara earlier.

They escort Rude Buay to the parking lot. Before getting to their vehicle he is partially knocked out. They drag him and toss him inside the trunk of their vehicle and drive off. Rude Buay struggles to stay in a conscious state of mind. But all he can see is a flashback to almost a year ago when Axel James and Ian Baynes, two members of the *Dragon Drug Cartel* tied him up and put him inside the trunk of their car and then drove him through the hills of Jamaica for the kill. Finally, the drug sets in and the agent snaps into a semi-unconscious state.

15

During the night Rude Buay sleeps like a baby in the private Jet aircraft manned by the *Dragon Drug Cartel*. The following morning, he wakes up in Nogales, Mexico. The airplane in which he was transported, touched down and taxied to a private hangar. They transport Rude Buay to a guest house strapped inside a customized van. This wooded building is located deep inside the rugged hills of Nogales, Mexico and overlooking the city.

Later, one of Alberto Gomez's guards drags Rude Buay from the guest room and, into the makeshift meeting room. There is a big table set in the middle of the room surrounded by six chairs. The aura inside that room is so tense; you can cut it with a knife.

Seated at the head of the table is Drug Czar Alberto Gomez. On his right in the anti-clockwise direction is his wife Denise Gomez. Next to Denise is seated, Shelly Hall. Marcus Ranks sits to her right. Next to Marcus and facing Alberto Gomez, is Miles Tate! Sitting next to Tate is Grace McCloud. And seated next to Grace is Sammy Chin.

The guard escorts Rude Buay to that vacant seat at the table next to Alberto Gomez. He plops the agent down on the chair.

The door, in two halves, swings open in unison. Two Hispanic men in male nurse attire enter, closing the door effortlessly behind them. One guard places a tray on the table in-front of Rude Buay and grinds his enormous bicuspids teeth. The other places a pair of pliers and a washcloth next to the tray and grunts *doh, ray, me, fah, soh, la, te, doh*. As if to say this is my song, soon we are going to kill you if ...,

Alberto Gomez presides:

"Welcome Agent Rude Buay!"

Rude Buay is still groggy but can still hear the echo of the last *doh*!

Alberto Gomez slaps Rude Buay in his face.

Rude Buay feels it. He evolves into an alert stance.

"Are you with us Rude Buay?"

Asks Alberto Gomez.

Rude Buay stares at him as his intellect drifts in and out like a rolling tide.

"It is imperative you remain alert during this meeting as this could determine if you should live or die."

Rude Buay nods in unconscious agreement.

"While we have your undivided attention, Rude Buay I might as well cut straight to the chase. I must let you know that you are a very lucky man, to still be alive. We could have had you killed but instead, we brought you to Nogales to allow you to team up with the fastest-growing cartel ever orchestrated. You are hard-working: meaning you get the job done. It would be beneficial to you and us both if you would team up with the organization as part of our extension program.

You would benefit from an unmatched salary. Plus receive bonuses from our annual profits. In the first year a whopping 5% will go to you, the second year 10%, the third year 15% and the fourth year 20%. I know how much you make as a U.S. D.E.A. I would say it's peanuts compared to what you can earn just on salary alone in the narcotics trade.

Rude Buay is hearing Alberto Gomez but he isn't assimilating nor digesting the team player mindset strategy or the Czars' monotonous trade philosophy.

"Basically, you will be working along with the border patrols acting as if you are completely on their side. We need an inside man on our side. You will let our dealers into the U.S. unscathed. If ever there is a sticky situation involving our men you will work it out in our favor. Of course with you being the head honcho you will step in and put out the fire. Our men are well trained they know the border lingo, even dealing with the meter maids on the other side they are adept. With you as the "top dog" we will be a force to be reckoned with.

It's no happenstance that the lead *Border Patrol Officer* position is open. With your credentials, you shouldn't have a problem nailing that prestigious job. The U.S. government would not turn you down; all you need to do is to apply. Look at what you've done for them. Your résumé speaks for itself, agent."

Rude Buay is somewhat flattered.

"You will fit in so well no one would even know you are working for us. After 5 years you can feel free to walk away, no strings attached!"

There is silence. All eyes are now focused on Rude Buay anticipating his acceptance of the deal. Instead, he composes himself but remains silent.

Alberto Gomez quickly states:

"If you refuse the job we'll have no choice but to execute you by hanging based on charges of treason, along with all the trouble you have caused us in the past. So while the noose waits to dangle for your neck at the gallows, those two gentlemen standing over you have been instructed to extract one of your fingernails daily, leaving your pinky fingers for the last days leading up to your hanging."

Once again all eyes are focused on Rude Buay expecting him to give in. Finally, he composes himself. *"The things I've been through give me fortitude. I'm not easily broken. Not only have I seen too much but I've been through too much. Selling out is not in my character. You may hang my body on that gallows but you will never hang my character!"*

States Rude Buay.

"I'll give you ten hours to think it over and come to an intelligent decision. The initial nail removal process could begin at sunrise tomorrow. First, they would start with your right thumb and then your trigger holding finger the next morning."

The meeting adjourns. Not before the *Dragon Drug Cartel* performs its freebasing *get-high* ritual.

16

It's almost sunrise the following morning and almost ten hours since the *Dragon Drug Cartel* wrapped their meeting with Agent Rude Buay. The agent still doesn't accept the offer to team up with the *Dragons*. So to put seasoned salt in Rude Buay's wounds the *Dragons* put Dr. Tamara Ross on a Jet bound from Jamaica to Nogales, Mexico. The objective: to arrange for her hanging before Rude Buay's trip to the gallows.

Dr. Ross has no idea what their plot is about. The flight crew speaks using codes. None of which is familiar to her.

BACK IN JAMAICA Banks shows up at *Sandals* as backup for agent Rude Buay. The traffic heading to *Sandals* was full of nothing but gridlock and bottlenecking. Somewhat slowed he arrived there late. Now he is surprised that he didn't get a progress report from Rude Buay.

Upon arrival on the hotel compound, Banks learns from his inside source at *Sandals* that Dr. Ross had been moved to a facility in Nogales, Mexico. His source an elderly woman had heard them speaking in Spanish and heard their planned destination for Dr. Ross. Also, that agent Rude Buay was seen accompanying two men to their car hours before.

Upon returning home Walter Banks gets a phone call from Chelo informing him that the *Dragons* had moved operations from Colombia and set up base in Nogales, Mexico; to better facilitate their Meth trade. Chelo and Walter Banks later pack up some of their spy gadgets in boxes and suitcases. They head out separately to the Arizona, Mexican border town of Nogales and later to Nogales, Mexico.

IMMEDIATELY AFTER SUNSET the following day, the door to agent Rude Buay's makeshift prison cell opens. The room is exactly 10 feet by 5 feet. Inside, there is a cot on one side against the wall. On the other side is a small wooden table on the other side. Next to the table is a small trash can. The dangling light bulb on a hanging electrical cord in the roof is illuminated. The two men, seen before dressing in a nurse's uniform, barge inside.

Rude Buay is lying on the cot with both hands and feet tied with nylon ropes.

One of the men is carrying a tray along with a large pair of pliers. The other man holds in his hands a small damp towel and a box of latex gloves. He is also wearing an apron. He passes a pair of transparent latex gloves to his partner, who puts them on methodically as if he's a surgeon getting ready to perform a special surgical operation.

Moments later the apron-wearing man grabs agent Rude Buay's hands. Together they tie down Rude Buay's right hand on the table, securing the ropes around the wooden table's legs.

Rude Buay knows what's about to go down any minute, he flinches not only in his mind, so does his body. The agent's right thumb is the main focus of the pair of pliers.

One attendant presses down on Rude Buay's right hand using both of his hands, while the other brutally removes the agent's right thumbnail using the pair of pliers. Rude Buay yells out as the pain surges through his entire body.

The thumbnail, with some flesh attached to it, gets deposited in the trash can. The attendant then uses the damp rag to wipe the blood from the table including the vast amount flowing from the agent's bleeding right thumb.

From inside his apron pocket, the attendant grabs a piece of bandage and wraps it around the nail-less thumb, tying it around the agent's other four fingers on that hand and tying it around the wrist.

Rude Buay is then escorted to the cot in his room. The two men finish cleaning up of the blood residue and depart.

The following evening at sunset they return and extract the thumb on his left hand. Each day for ten days, these men remove one of Rude Buay's fingernails leaving those on his two pinky fingers for last as ordered by Alberto Gomez.

17

With the ten-day fingernails removal ordeal completed, Rude Buay remains all drenched with blood, as blood from his ten fingers drains into a cloth bag wrapped around both of his hands like a muzzle. The bag is tied at the wrists. The two men dressed in bloodied nurse uniforms strap Rude Buay onto a truck. Before they send Rude Buay to the gallows they ask the agent what he would like before he dies.

"I would like to see Dr. Tamara Ross again."

Says Rude Buay.

Attempting to get the agent to buy into the team concept of the *Dragons* for one last time and avoid being hanged, Alberto Gomez requests a laptop computer brought to the truck with video clips of Tamara. The two male attendants bring out the laptop and show Rude Buay video clips of Tamara being beaten and spat upon by several Mexican maids.

The videos, very horrifying and are more than what the agent wanted as a dying wish. He tugs at the ropes to escape but is restrained by the two men.

In the interim, the driver arrives and checks the truck along with the ropes, which binds Rude Buay, to ensure the agent is securely tied up.

The truck departs during the wee hours of the morning as the clouds begin to give way to the sunrise in Nogales hills. Alberto Gomez, Denise Gomez, Miles Tate, Shelly Hall, Marcus Ranks, Grace McCloud, Sammy Chin, and the two male attendants celebrate during an intense freebasing event in the upper room of the *Casa*. At this meeting, Alberto Gomez also introduces newcomer Victor Crip a Mexican native in his mid-30s to head up operations in Nogales - the position which Rude Buay had recently turned down.

As part of Victor's initiation, the *newbie* pulls out a glass pipe, similar to a crack pipe. He pours in about 0.2 grams of methamphetamine. Holding the pipe on his lips, he starts to gently heat the bottom part of the pipe to allow the drug to vaporize. He slowly inhales. He passes the pipe along with the crystal meth folded in an aluminum foil. The others partake in the *chasing of the white dragon*, a term used amongst drug dealers for meth smoking. They all are now as high as kites. They laugh and cut up detailing what Rude Buay will say and do as the noose tightens around his neck.

Rude Buay couldn't help but hear and notice their taunting from the window across the way as he is driven to his hanging by the Mexican truck driver. In a celebratory and festive mood, the drug lords synchronize their watches; as the hanging was set for 9:00 AM sharp.

CHELO HAD ARRIVED IN NOGALES, MEXICO on the afternoon of the previous day before the scheduled hanging and set up his spy operations in that city. After working tirelessly rigging several antennas from his wooden hut, he was able to pinpoint the location where agent Rude Buay was detained by the *Dragons*. On foot, he hustled to the area. Everyone was still asleep at the *Casa*.

Later the truck took off and subsequently made its way through the rolling hills and dirt roads of Nogales, Mexico. The journey continued as multitudes of vulture swarmed overhead sweeping down momentarily to feed on the remains of human bodies littered like a mass execution through the hills. Rude

Buay had never been to war in this country but imagined that at least they buried the bodies. The milieu was horrific! The hissing musical sound of maggots indicated that no graves were prepared for those who perished, not even trenches. The stench is overbearing, to say the least.

The truck finally stops on top of the hill close to the gallows. From that vantage point, one could see a swinging noose awaiting the agent. Two men dressed in coveralls await his arrival: One to hang him and the other standing next to the grave to bury him in that seven-footer open shallow trench. The driver steps out focused on the task at hand.

Chelo takes a portion out of the page from the book by Walter Banks who had rescued him when he was driven to the gallows in Colombia over a year ago. Chelo promptly unties himself from underneath the truck's chassis and swiftly kicks the driver in his lower stomach region. The driver falls over gasping for air. As a result of the blow, the driver's rifle falls and is lying on the ground. Chelo kicks the rifle in Rude Buay's direction. Both of Rude Buay's hands are still muzzled in that bloodied cloth sack. Using his teeth the agent speedily unties the sack and crawls on his stomach and elbows towards the fallen rifle.

The barefooted Chelo kicks the driver one more time. This time he kicks him hard in his stomach. The driver once again crouches and gasps continuously for air.

Forgetting how painful it could be losing all ten fingernails in less than two weeks, Rude Buay picks up the rifle, forces his bloodied swollen trigger finger inside the trigger slot. It bleeds as he pulls the switch. He blasts the driver.

The hanger and the undertaker both hear the sound of that single gunshot and depart speedily from around the hanging site. The undertaker drops his shovel in the process. It falls into the trench. They race to the truck which transported Rude Buay to the *set*.

Rude Buay shoots again and kills both men while Chelo positions himself as a decoy. Chelo and Rude Buay hurry on their feet.

Moments later, after their departure, the truck in which Rude Buay was transported explodes at exactly 9:05 AM into a ball of fire.

Now free, Chelo and Rude Buay continue on foot for many hours through the rugged hillsides of Nogales.

CHELO, EARLIER before the truck was scheduled to leave for the gallows, ever alert; while under the truck's chassis, and waiting for it to depart from the *Casa*; was fortunate to eavesdrop on the conversations of the two male attendants. They had mentioned Tamara's whereabouts about two miles away from the *Casa*. Also, that she was next on the list to be hanged and that she was supposed to be hanged before Rude Buay but Alberto Gomez had wanted to welcome in

Victor Crip with the hanging of Rude Buay on the following day instead. They had even articulated about her beauty and implied doing a twosome or a *watch while I do it* with her if time permitted. They even joked about the latter and suggested tossing a coin upon arrival for supremacy. Immediately after their conversation, Chelo was able to pick up this house where Tamara resided on his pen radar.

Now, he and Rude Buay move swiftly in that direction through Southern Nogales.

The terrain is a rough one through the hills, more so for Rude Buay not exposed to that mode of getting around since his days in elementary school when he sometimes went to school barefooted. Chelo, though on barefoot can deal with the blisters and bruises to his feet. Rude Buay still in those shoes, he wore to locate Tamara back at Sandals in Jamaica, has at this point almost worn them out. Their soles give way leaving him with not only multiple calluses but severe bruises and blisters as well. The thorns from failed cactus add their punch to the feet of both men.

While traveling through the hills they discover many chopped up dismembered bodies as vultures continue to feed and the unpleasant odor surfaces. The stench remains unbearable, coming from the corpses made up of men and women and children and celebrated by maggots. Even so, they must hurry as time elapse and the already high stakes increase. Rude Buay falls

between some waist-high shrubbery but gets up and
continues tirelessly.

18

Nearing the house a small dog begins barking as Rude Buay and Chelo closes in on the domicile. A guard keeping watch is alerted and trains his weapon on Rude Buay and Chelo for several minutes accompanied by dogs. The guard's gun runs out of bullets after an extensive cat and mouse ordeal. Now, the switch flips. Rude Buay, on a foot race, is in pursuit of the guard. The dogs cool it wagging their tails. Using his rifle he cuts down the guard whose dodging skill and agility on foot-speed runs out. He enters the house in take-down style with Chelo in tow.

Inside he discovers Dr. Tamara Ross. She is tied up hands and feet kneeling at the bedside. Chelo finds a kitchen knife and quickly cuts the ropes. Together the trio journey into the city and takes refuge in a hotel after sundown. The following morning at sunrise Chelo says his goodbyes to Rude Buay and Tamara.

TAMARA PROCEEDS TO BANDAGE-UP Rude Buay's ten nail-less fingers and attends to his gunshot wound suffered in Shanghai. The regular program on the TV is interrupted as the reporter comes on with breaking news:

"Almost two dozen kids under the ages of 12 and involved in the trade of Methamphetamine were involved in yet another standoff with border patrols in Nogales, Arizona earlier today. As a result, many officers were left dead and more than half of those kids were captured and their AK47s confiscated. However, the other kids fled to safety through the Mexican, Nogales hillsides. Mexican police are now combing through the desert looking for these bandits. More news to come on this evolving story."

Rude Buay asks,

"What's up with these kids?" They have no epiphany as to what they are into."

"Not only that,"

Says Dr. Ross.

"What's your take on Meth?"

Asks Rude Buay.

Dr. Tamara Ross voices her concern:

"You lost your cousin and his daughter."

"Don't remind me,"

Says Rude Buay.

She continues,

"According to the National Institute on Drug and Abuse, National Institutes of Health in regards to how Meth affects the Brain and the Body:

No matter how methamphetamine is used, it eventually ends up that it can affect lots of brain structures but the ones it affects the most are the ones that contain a chemical called dopamine. The reason for this is that the shape, size, and chemical structure of methamphetamine and dopamine are similar. Before I tell you more about dopamine and methamphetamine, I'd better tell you how nerve cells work.

Rude Buay is all ears.

The human brain is made up of billions of nerve cells (or neurons). Neurons come in all shapes and sizes, but most have three important parts: a cell body that contains the nucleus and directs the activities of the neuron; dendrites, short fibers that receive messages from other neurons and relay them to the cell body; and an axon, a long single fiber that carries messages from the cell body to dendrites of other neurons.

Axons of one neuron and the dendrites of a neighboring neuron are located very close to each other, but they don't touch. Therefore, to communicate with each other they use chemical messengers known as neurotransmitters. When one neuron wants to send a message to another neuron it releases a neurotransmitter from its axon into the small space that separates the two neurons. This space is called a synapse. The neurotransmitter crosses the synapse and attaches to specific places on the dendrites of the neighboring neuron called receptors. Once the neurotransmitter has relayed its message, it is either destroyed or taken back up into the first neuron where it is recycled for use again."

Rude Buay senses that Dr. Ross is on a roll and chooses not to interrupt the flow of such vital information but nods to assure her that he's still listening.

"There are many different neurotransmitters, but the one that is most affected by methamphetamine is dopamine. Dopamine is sometimes called the pleasure neurotransmitter because it helps you feel good from things like playing soccer, eating a big piece of chocolate cake, or riding a roller coaster. When something pleasurable happens, certain axons release lots of dopamine. The dopamine attaches to receptors on dendrites of neighboring neurons and passes on the pleasure message.

This process is stopped when dopamine is released from the receptors and pumped back into the neuron that released it where it is stored for later use.

Usually, neurons recycle dopamine. But methamphetamine can fool neurons into taking it up just like they would dopamine. Once inside a neuron, methamphetamine causes that neuron to release lots of dopamine. All these dopamine causes the person to feel an extra sense of pleasure that can last all day. But eventually, these pleasurable effects stop. They are followed by unpleasant feelings called a "crash" that often lead a person to use more of the drug. If a person continues to use methamphetamine, they will have a difficult time feeling pleasure from anything. Imagine no longer enjoying your favorite food or an afternoon with your friends!

Methamphetamine has lots of other effects:

Because it is similar to dopamine, methamphetamine can change the function of any neuron that contains dopamine. And if this weren't enough, methamphetamine can also affect neurons that contain two other neurotransmitters called serotonin and norepinephrine. All of this means that methamphetamine can change how lots of things in the brain and the bodywork.

Even small amounts of methamphetamine can cause a person to be more awake and active, lose their appetite, and become irritable and aggressive. Methamphetamine also causes a person's blood pressure to increase and their heart to beat faster."

(She pauses for breath and then continues)
Long Term Effects of Meth:

Scientists are using brain imaging techniques, like positron emission tomography (called PET for short), to study the brains of human methamphetamine users. They have

93

discovered that even three years after long-time methamphetamine users had quit using the drug, their dopamine neurons were still damaged. Scientists don't know yet whether this damage is permanent, but this research shows that changes in the brain from methamphetamine use can last a long time. Research with animals has shown that the drug methamphetamine can also damage neurons that contain serotonin. This damage also continues long after the drug use is stopped.

These changes in dopamine and serotonin neurons may explain some of the effects of methamphetamine. If a person uses methamphetamine for a long time, they may become paranoid. They may also hear and see things that aren't there. These are called hallucinations. Because methamphetamine causes big increases in blood pressure, someone using it for a long time may also have permanent damage to blood vessels in the brain. This can lead to strokes caused by bleeding in the brain.

Tamara **adds:**
Researchers are only beginning to understand how methamphetamine acts in the brain and body. When they learn more about how methamphetamine causes its effects, they may be able to develop treatments that prevent or reverse the damage this drug can cause."
"Really?"
Asks Rude Buay as he picks up his car keys and automatic rifle.

"That's why Glenda at an unconscious level and state of mind walked onto the Freeway and committed suicide by having that eighteen-wheeler run her over and Glen later blew out his brains,"
Says Rude Buay.
"She must have been so brain-dead, her body had to follow its leader,"
Informs Tamara Ross.
"Thanks for the research. Maybe someday you'll make the next breakthrough."
Says Rude Buay.
 He kisses Tamara on her lips as he walks towards the door.
"They can't stop you! You're **UNSTOPPABLE**, you're **UNTOUCHABLE** but most of all … Randy, you're *SHATTERPROOF*!!!"
Proclaims Tamara to Rude Buay.
He slips two pairs of ventilated gloves provided by Tamara over the fresh bandage on his five fingers of both hands. Rude Buay makes his exit from the hotel room door in terminator style.
"I'll get you out of here soon!"

19

The Methamphetamine trade continues to expand rapidly, not only in Mexico and Arizona but has also diversified to Jamaica, Asia, Los Angeles, New York as well as the U.S./Canadian border. Several dominant cartels including the *Dragons* and the *Sinaloa Cartel* compete viciously for drug territory resulting in many killings, particularly in Mexico.

Many traders in Mexico distribute the drug on multiple levels of trade. Chelo, one day while collecting video feed through his high tech satellite equipment discovered what Rude Buay later described as one of the most successful and amazing ways, though on a small scale, to smuggle drugs across the border.

The *Dragons* smuggled narcotics through these tunnels from Mexico to Arizona every day including Saturday, Sundays and Holidays.

Methamphetamine smugglers in the border town of Nogales, Mexico continue to bring drugs into the U.S. through Nogales, Arizona, as some would say *for the cost of a quarter*.

They habitually use parking meters on International Street, which hugs the border fence in Nogales: These meters cost 25 cents. So the smugglers in Mexico would tunnel under the fence and wind up under the metered parking spaces. There they would carefully cut neat rectangle type manholes out of the pavement. Their associates in Nogales would park false-bottomed vehicles in the spaces above the holes, feed the meters, and then wait while the underground smugglers stuffed their cars full of Meth and other narcotics from below. This was done multiple times per day.

As soon as this exchange was finished, the smugglers use jacks to put the pavement *plugs* back into the manholes. The cars then drive away loaded with a variety of narcotics, mainly methamphetamine.

Additionally, some smugglers were caught on video using catapults which launched bales of drugs across the border fence. If it was going to get across the border those Mexicans found a way.

Methamphetamine became very popular also in Jamaica even though the effects of Glenda Bascombe's death were still felt and talked about by many during their daily routines whether on the street or in their homes. To many concerned parents, it stuck out like a sore thumb.

IT IS WELL KNOWN INSIDE the drug world that the cartels control the trafficking of drugs from South America to the U.S., a business that is worth an estimated $13billion (£9 billion) a year. Their power grew as the U.S. stepped up anti-narcotics operations in the Caribbean and Florida. A U.S. state department report estimated that as much as 90% of all cocaine and methamphetamine consumed in the US comes via Mexico.

Meanwhile, many are killed both in Mexico and neighboring U.S. border towns like Nogales by the *Dragon Drug Cartel,* not only as of the demands for narcotics increase but also because smugglers fail to carry out their assignment and creditors fail to pay up for their drugs.

The Mexican government issued partial figures on 11 January 2012. These showed that 12,903 people had been killed in violence blamed on organized crime from January to September 2011. Added to the previous overall total, this means that 47,515 people had died in the five years of Mr. Calderon's presidency. Although there is no breakdown, the victims include suspected drug gang members, members of the security forces and those considered innocent bystanders.

Reported one source,

While another source stated:

Violence was first concentrated in Mexico's northern border regions, especially Chihuahua, as well as Pacific states like Sinaloa, Michoacán and Guerrero. Ciudad Juarez (just across from El Paso in Texas) was the most violent city. In 2010, some 3,100 people were killed in Juarez, which has a population of more than a million.

But since 2010, violence has spread to other regions, including Nuevo Leon and Tamaulipas states. One of the focal points for violence has been Mexico's third-largest city, Monterrey.

The year 2011 also saw new areas hit. For example, VeraCrip on the eastern coast saw a series of mass killings.

The Government of Mexico feels the police cannot be trusted. Drug cartels with massive resources at their disposal have repeatedly managed to infiltrate the underpaid police, from the grassroots level to the very top. Efforts are underway to rebuild the entire structure of the Mexican police force, but the process is expected to take years.

RUMORS SPREAD QUICKLY in Jamaica amongst Rude Buays' peers that the agent was still alive and stationed in Mexico fighting the war on drugs. Meanwhile, many Jamaicans, as well as meth users, were becoming mentally paralyzed from the use of Methamphetamine. Jamaica was rising rapidly in the meth using stats.

Commissioner Richard Baptiste, in his 50s, and Mildred Simms, who had previously teamed up with Rude Buay in Jamaica and China against the *Dragons*, for a while believed that the agent Rude Buay had turned his back on his people.

Mildred Simms and the Commissioner also accused Rude Buay of forsaking his Jamaican people when they faced similar drug problems. *Tivoli Gardens* stated: was like a simmering volcano and could erupt again spewing out many more Johnny *Too Bads*.

Not sure how to handle this dilemma, they even took things a step further to discuss the elimination proceedings of Rude Buay with the Governor-General of Jamaica Bradford Wiley.

In this plot they would secretly deliver Rude Buay into the hands of the *Dragon Drug Cartel*, just like the Philistines, in the *Bible* days did to Samson.

Even so, Governor-General Wiley, a man of peace and tranquility saw things differently and suggested to both the Commissioner and Mildred Simms that they team up with Rude Buay to fight against the *Dragons*. His wisdom led him to believe that Rude Buay was about "One Love for Jamaica."

Was that enough to change their perspective on the Rude Buay's situation? At least they let it rest for a while as they came to grips with convincing themselves that if Rude Buay was involved it had to be a worthwhile cause not only for Jamaicans but the whole world.

20

A dark-colored jeep speeds through the dirt road surrounded by trees and shrubbery in the hillsides of Nogales, Mexico. A blanket of dust follows it in tow. Finally, the vehicle comes to a halt on top of a hill overlooking Nogales close to the Mexican/U.S. border. Another jeep is parked on top of that hill.

Out of the newly arrived vehicle, step out Denise Gomez, Shelly Hall, and Grace McCloud. The three women are dangerously armed with rifles. They move towards the other parked jeep.

Inside that parked vehicle is Victor Crip the newly appointed drug lord to oversee trade between the twin cities of Nogales. Using his binoculars Crip surveys the border. Noticing the three *femme Fatales,* Crip discards his binoculars and picks up his semi-automatic. He senses some rivalry. The women continue to aggressively pursue Victor Crip with aimed rifles. He now senses more than ever his life being threatened. He notices their dragon tattoo signature. He knows them.

"*¿Cómo eta?* What's up, ladies? We are on the same team."

Crip addresses,

No one responds verbally, neither in Spanish nor English. Instead, they maintain their stance with weapons pointed at him.

"Mistaken identity? We work for the same boss. Are you *locas*?"

He questions.

"What's up with the Nogales shipment?"

Asks Denise.

"That's right! The Nogales shipment?"

Restates Shelly Hall,

"*Muchos problemas señoritas.* The Blackman! The Blackman! Let me explain."

Says Victor Crip.

"Explain?"

Asks Grace McCloud.

Denise continues,

"Do you see all the cars parked on meters over on Independence Street? They have been there all day. If those drivers run out of quarters to feed those meters, do you know we could come up against the *policia*? If we fail in getting them to accept a bribe, they will instantly shut down our tunnel meter operation."

"That's right! Los Angeles and Canada are still waiting for their supply of Meth. You are pissing off Miles Tate. Who thinks we are dropping the ball!"

Says Shelly Hall.

Victor Crip looks at his pair of binoculars on the floor of the jeep with its driver's door still ajar. He then looks at the women still maintaining their offensive stance.

"You are causing problems on Independence Street, Victor Crip."

Says Grace McCloud,

"What were you looking at inside that gadget when we showed up? *Shades of...*? You are not doing your job. Goddammit!"

"*Dios* made the man and he made the woman. If you all will let me speak, I can certainly explain."

"And your name is JESUS?"

Asks Grace McCloud.

"No. I was looking through those binoculars for a black man carrying a rifle and sporting a scorpion tattoo.

RUDE BUAY VOL. III

Didn't you hear? Last night they said he shot up the tires on all the eighteen-wheelers heading for the parking lot and then called in the police who made several arrests. We don't have his full identity. The only evidence is that he is black and had a rifle according to one of our drivers who made his getaway."

"Why the heck weren't we notified? Did you inform Alberto Gomez?" We could have already caught the bastard. On the other hand, I think you are dreaming."

Says Shelly Hall.

"I just got the word so I decided to find that man before he strikes again. I want to kill him myself."

Says Victor Crip.

The women re-board their jeep and drive back down the hill and on their way back into the hills and into Mexico.

MOMENTS LATER, Rude Buay on the other side of the hill, oblivious of the fact that Victor Crip has visitors in the form of Hall and Gomez kept crawling on his stomach toward the summit. He finally gets a glimpse of Victor outside his jeep looking through the binoculars. Victor's back is turned in the direction of the agent as he is focused on binocular surveillance.

Rude Buay whistles out and then throw a rock at Victor Crip. As soon as the drug lord turns around and is now facing Rude Buay, the agent caps him with several rounds while still lying on his stomach. He then gets up out of the fetal position and rummages through Victor Crip's jeep. Rude Buay discovers at least 30 pounds of Meth, two rifles, stacks of U.S. one hundred dollar bills, freebasing utensils, along with twenty kilos of uncut cocaine.

Additionally, agent Rude Buay confiscates Crip's binoculars and his jeep.

Using his elbow to steer the vehicle the agent departs speedily down the hill.

21

While returning to the base of the hill Rude Buay's phone rings. He fumbles to retrieve it from inside the pocket of his pullover jacket and does. It's Heidi Hudson. He immediately senses a sparkle in her voice. She is upbeat. Was she looking forward to once again connecting with her true partner in crime?

"Rude Buay, where the heck are you?"
She inquires.

"Nogales, Mexico,"
He responds.
"I will be joining you shortly even if it costs me my
J O B. Ortiz was not happy with me asking for the time
off. He suspected I was going to be teaming up with
you and didn't look too happy."
Says Hudson.
"Very Interesting. Hit me up when you land."
Says Rude Buay, as he hangs up.

THE FOLLOWING MORNING Heidi Hudson arrives
in Nogales, Mexico and meets the battered Rude Buay
near his hotel across the way from Independence
Street.
Noticing his swollen hands, and most noticeably the
fight inside of him not being realized brings tears to
her eyes. She gets on the phone after shedding some
tears and connects with their other Jamaican allies.

IN MEXICO AND ITS BORDER TOWNS, the word
spreads that a black man using a rifle shot up several
tractor-trailers carrying Meth to be distrusted through
the border tunnels. The cartel senses that it is Rude
Buay but doubts that he could have escaped the
hanging much less the vehicular explosion. Alberto
Gomez, Miles Tate, Denise Gomez, Shelly Hall, and the
others are very confused as it has been reported that

the man sports a scorpion tattoo like the one displayed by Rude Buay.

Also, upon learning about the death of Victor Crip, yet another mystery is created for them; they recently discovered Crip's corpse in the Nogales hills.

While the *Dragons* look for the mysterious Blackman, the Mexico *policia* looks for more evidence regarding the tunnel drug transporting operation. They not only tow away several vehicles from Independence Street but discover that these vehicles were equipped with a manhole in the floor to pick up drugs from suppliers through underground tunnels with manholes and deliver them to dealers ready to transport them across the U.S., Canada, and China. Several arrests were made.

The following day city workers in Nogales embark upon sealing off those manholes and tunnels used as conduits for smugglers to transport drugs across the Mexican border into Arizona.

LATER THAT EVENING, Mildred, the Police Commissioner, and Banks; who have been searching tirelessly in Mexico for Rude Buay; arrive in the Mexican city of Nogales. They finally meet up with agent Heidi Hudson, Chelo, and Rude Buay in a small hotel suite and orchestrate a plan of attack to further counteract the *Dragon Drug Cartel*. At this meeting which, in more ways than one is like an ally reunion,

Rude Buay talks about the harmful effects of Methamphetamine on the human brain and body. Some key points in the research delivered by Tamara bear weight in his speech. Additionally, also how they were going to stop the *Dragons* by destroying their Mexican strongholds. The main objective: to decrease the number of drugs flowing out of Mexico to the U.S. and other countries as well. In the words of Rude Buay: "We will not only cripple but we will freeze the trade." So they divide, and team up, to conquer. Agent Heidi Hudson teams up with the veteran agent Walter Banks, Mildred Simms teams up with the Jamaican Police Commissioner Richard Baptiste and Rude Buay teams up with Chelo.

Walter Banks and Heidi Hudson were paired up not too long ago in Jamaica so that chemistry was tight. Mildred Simms and Richard Baptiste had also worked together when Rude Buay first fought against the *Dragons* in Jamaica. They had also worked together for the Jamaican government in Port Antonio. So they all were in sync.

Rude Buay felt obligated to mentor Chelo and pass the baton to the man who risked his life to save his. Everyone had been in this warfare before except for Chelo; he had never used a gun.

In three separate jeeps, all six officials pack up multiple guns and other weapons of mass destruction.

Immediately they take to the streets of Nogales, Mexico.

22

With the death of the newly appointed Victor Crip, the *Dragon Drug Cartel* was now without a key person to head up their drug smuggling operation at the Mexico/Nogales border. Plus, the word was out that agent Rude Buay could still be alive except none of the Dragons had seen him. So they turned down the rumor about his existence.

Alberto Gomez their leader was already heavily taxed with the global expansion of the *Dragon Cartel,* so he required a quality replacement in Mexico.

IT IS NOW 10:15 PM IN CHINA. Exactly 15 minutes after the lockdown at the Shanghai Central Prison. All heads are accounted for except Salvador. The Colombian chemist and Drug Lord who worked previously for the *Dragon Drug Cartel* and imprisoned less than 3 months ago is missing. He was initially arrested, charged and sentenced after over ten thousand cans of milk packed with uncut cocaine were discovered inside a submarine down the Chinese river bound for the Caribbean. The estimated street value of the cargo was over $10M. Salvador was already serving a portion of that 10-year sentence.

Outside the prison gate and up the street, Salvador, in a warden uniform, boards a waiting taxi. The taxi takes off.

About over an hour before prison lockdown and a few minutes after dinner, Salvador whisked away from the prison yard to the men's room.

Earlier that day after a phone conversation initiated by Alberto Gomez, Salvador accessed the warden's office and stole a uniform carelessly sitting inside the warden's closet. He placed it inside a black plastic trash bag and stored it at the bottom of the men's restroom trash can.

Before lockdown and after dinner, Salvador changed into that uniform and boldly walked out of the prison. The guard on duty waved to Salvador as he exited.

Oblivious that he was not the warden whose name tag was prominently displayed on his jacket.

Alberto Gomez had already arranged to have a taxi waiting for Salvador after lockdown.

Salvador was whisked away to the airport. There he met a woman who handed him a plane ticket, fake IDs and a duffel bag. Salvador went to the men's room and changed into civilian clothing, breezed through security and boarded an aircraft heading to Mexico. The following day he arrived in Nogales, Mexico.

Upon Salvador's arrival Drug Czar and leader of the *Dragon Drug Cartel*, Alberto Gomez quickly appointed the Colombian chemist, better known as Sal to head up the Nogales/Mexico border. The position which agent Rude Buay had turned down.

Sal had been known for creating the Dragon X brand of cocaine in Colombia. This brand was the result of a glitch. One mixed with cyanide and responsible for killing several Jamaican kids almost a year ago. Sal was also the point person who assisted David Lee, the Chinese drug lord in the packaging of cocaine wrapped in Ziploc bags and shipped in milk cartons. This narcotics shipment strategy caused the death of many, including little Leticia the 3-year-old Jamaican girl.

As the man in charge of the Methamphetamine operation in Mexico, the *Dragons* had put in place not only a chemist but a hard-working individual in the person of Salvador. He was not only loyal to Alberto Gomez but dedicated to his cause: growing the cartel into a global operation. On several occasions Alberto Gomez reminded Sal: *We will not only expand across the five oceans but will cause some of the most devastating recalls that country* (referring to the U.S.) *has ever experienced.*

Salvador bought into that concept.

CHELO, USING HIS LAPTOP connected to his satellites and hidden cameras, which was recently set up in Nogales along the Mexican border and elsewhere. By doing so he was able to eavesdrop on the *Dragons.*

The cartel also positioned itself in Vermont close to the U.S./Canadian border. At that location, they used an old warehouse as a depot. The eighteen-wheelers would pull up, bound from Mexico. Then transfer their cargo inside waiting vans.

These were customized vans usually manned by two or three people. They would load up their Meth supply onto the vans and head for the Canadian border. The border patrols on the Canadian side would do minimal checking of these vehicles operated by Canadians. So these Meth smugglers got away scot-free. It was said that the ex-agent Miles Tate, a Miami native, had this drug smuggling operation locked down. Meth sales soared in Canada as a result of his involvement.

Grace McCloud has filled the void left by the deceased Frankie O'Neal, Johnny *Too Bad*, Amanda Kingsley and Agnes Richards in Miami. This city situated in south Florida serves as a hub not only for the southern states but the Caribbean as well. Their shipments came through the Mexico/El Paso border on eighteen-wheelers. Products were unloaded and stored in a warehouse similar to the previously owned *Milky Way*. Marcus Ranks headed up the Tivoli Gardens/Port Antonio operations in Jamaica. Their shipments came through the Mexico/El Paso border on eighteen-wheelers via Miami and were sent out in small ships into Jamaica via Port Antonio and Ocho Rios.

Ever since Rude Buay, and most recently his team, began concentrating on combating the trade of narcotics in Mexico, Ranks had some room to trade freely and became stellar at smuggling Meth along with other narcotics products into Jamaica. He was too clever for Jamaican law enforcement. In other words, he was slippery. A relative of Johnny *Too Bad*, Ranks had a vendetta not only against the U.S. but against Drug Enforcement Agencies as well.

OVERSEAS, IN CHINA Sammy Chin tied the knot with the imprisoned widow of the deceased drug lord David Lee. With Lee's empire shattered and now in the rebuilding stage, his widow Chu Ling became a great fit for Sammy Chin. The only downfall was: even though she was an adept drug dealer who unfortunately got busted, she had to operate from behind prison walls. Palladium on Chu Ling was very tight. Serving mostly as a referral source for Chin, was her main contribution to the trade. Chu Ling was determined to be in the thick of things very soon. Thus, giving China that clout it once had when her previous husband David Lee was alive and ran the narcotics trade.

RUDE BUAY AND CHELO followed in tow by Walter Banks and Heidi Hudson, accompanied by Mildred Simms and Richard Baptiste, pull up outside an abandoned warehouse in Mexico a few miles from Nogales, the neighboring town in Arizona. The agents are poised. They, survey from their vehicle and gather satellite feed posted at the border.

23

While the agents waited undetected in their vehicles parked between the trees located above the warehouse, several tractor-trailers pull up and enter the warehouse. The agents waited for them to exit the building but they never did. So the agents moved in ensuing an investigation and a possible drug sting. Upon arrival, the more than six eighteen-wheelers had all vanished. The loading docks were empty as well as the back parking lot. Rude Buay familiar with disappearance tactics used by the *Dragons* reflects on the disappearances of Johnny *Too Bad* and

Frankie O'Neal at a Manor in Miami several months prior. So the agent perceives and pursues a possible underground tunnel getaway.

Moments later all six agents find themselves driving through a long extended tunnel. In less than 15 minutes they wind up in another warehouse, this time across the borderline into Nogales, Arizona. That fleet of eighteen-wheelers is still nowhere to be found, not even a trace.

Rude Buay is also very cognizant of the fact that this tunnel had been used by the *Dragon Drug Cartel* to transport narcotics from Mexico into the U.S. He had seen the underground tunnel which was built underneath that manor in Miami.

Moments later Rude Buay gets on the phone with Michael Ortiz. Both men discuss the possible ways of freezing tunnel narcotics traffic to the U.S. Later that day U.S. Border Patrols surround that same warehouse in Nogales and with the aid of heavy-duty equipment they put up roadblocks to stop further tunnel traffic into the U.S.

As the news spreads, U.S. Border officials beef up border security to curtail any other tunneling from Mexico into the U.S.

THROUGH THE CALCULATED surveillance efforts of Chelo, Rude Buay learns that Salvador had arrived in Mexico and was filling the void left by the executed Victor Crip. So he and the agents embark on a mission to find Salvador. Rude Buay and Chelo cover the Mexican side of the border while Banks, Hudson, Simms, and Baptiste cover the town of Nogales, Arizona. With the disappearance of those eighteen-wheelers, they decide that they would beef up their security as well as their investigation.

Rude Buay and Chelo later return to Mexico through the same tunnel. On their way back they meet with an eighteen-wheeler coming straight ahead at them as if pursuing a head-on collision. Rude Buay manages to shoot at the driver and blowing out the front windscreen. The driver is untouched by that round. However, he tiers the truck on the right side of the tunnel while Rude Buay's jeep squeezes by on the left.

Rude Buay's jeep comes to a stop. The driver of the eighteen-wheeler truck gets out and starts shooting at Rude Buay and Chelo. They retaliate with several rounds of their own. The cat and mouse duel continues for several minutes inside the dark unlit tunnel. Finally, the driver takes off on foot through the tunnel and heading towards Mexico.

Chelo, excellent on foot leads the way in the foot race with Rude Buay following closely behind him.

The driver shoots again at the two agents. This time once again, only training his weapon.

Rude Buay get a shot off that sends the driver to the ground, another round finishes him off. After a search of the driver, his truck was searched, over 100 kilos of uncut cocaine was discovered in addition to large quantities of Methamphetamine and other narcotics inside the trailer. After calling in the *Policia* Rude Buay and Chelo leave the scene in pursuit of more *Dragons*.

LATER THAT DAY after receiving the news, Salvador consults with Alberto Gomez about the roadblocks placed by DEA inside the tunnel and impeding the flow of drugs to the U.S. along with the sting carried out on the now-deceased truck driver. Alberto Gomez, not only wondered who was behind this operation but set out to capture them. First, he thought it was the border patrols but knew he had been operating this way for several months and they had not caught on. So he ruled them out.

He thought about the U.S. DEA. But he knew without the experienced agent Rude Buay in their camp, they were playing major catch up. Although he had heard that a black man took Victor Crip's life, in his mind he knew that he had sent Rude Buay to the gallows. Additionally, to ensure the successful execution of his task, he had also backed up that expedition with a bomb attached to the truck carrying the agent to the gallows. So he ruled out the Rude Buay comeback scenario.

Could it have been Rude Buay's allies? Alberto Gomez knew they were not as efficient without the man who he so badly wanted on his team. So he sent Salvador on a rampage to bring in whoever it was that was raining on his Mexican global parade.

Rude Buay had previously equipped Chelo with a semi-automatic gun but was concerned about the bare-footedness of the man who had saved his life. Knowing how treacherous the search for the *Dragons* could become through the rugged hills of Nogales. So he pulls up at a shoe store and steps inside to purchase a pair of comfortable shoes for his sidekick. Planning to surprise Chelo, later on, he puts the pair of moccasins in a shopping bag and returns to his jeep. To his surprise, the jeep is there but Chelo and the laptop are missing.

24

When ex-agent Miles Tate learned that Chelo had been captured by the *Dragons* in Mexico, he travels from Vermont, where he had been stationed to be a part of the interrogation. He had already passed on U.S. D.E.A. secrets to Alberto Gomez, leader of the *Dragon Drug Cartel*. This opportunity would not only make him look good in Alberto Gomez's eyes but give him a chance to get some firsthand information from the man who had spied on the cartel from Colombia for many years. Tate was stoked!

Upon arriving in Mexico, Tate was met by Sal, the newly appointed Drug Lord to head up that region, also the man responsible for capturing Chelo. Alberto Gomez wanted to be in on the proceedings so he immediately flew into Mexico from China.

The interrogation was set for an office inside an abandoned warehouse in Nogales, Mexico. Chelo who looked somewhat battered was brought into the room that morning bound with ropes. Accompanied by two guards, they seat him on a chair in the middle of the room. Tied to the wooden chair which permitted him any but no movement or else the chair moved with him, Chelo sensed that his fate was going to be decided. He was not sure if they knew he was responsible for Rude Buay's escape. If they did, he envisioned not escaping, and being either hung from the gallows or executed.

Alberto Gomez and Salvador looked on while Miles Tate began with the *digging* process.

"Good morning Chelo!"

"Morning,"

Responds Chelo.

"Where do you live Chelo?"

"Bogota, Colombia,"

Replies Chelo.

"What brings you to Mexico? You've been here for some time now."

"D.E.A. business,"

Reveals Chelo.

"Who is your affiliation?"

"The U.S. government,"

Chelo responds.

"So you were brought in from Colombia to spy on the *Dragon Drug Cartel*?"

"I was brought here to work..."

Counters Chelo.

"Who brought you into Mexico?"

Interrupts Miles Tate.

"The D.E.A.,"

Says Chelo.

"Who...? Banks? Ortiz? Who do you report to?"

Asks Miles Tate.

"The D.E.A.,"

Answers Chelo.

"Is Rude Buay alive?"

"I don't know."

"You are such a liar. Which of those men, that I've just mentioned, do you report to?"

Asks Miles Tate.

"None of them. I report to the headquarters,"

Says Chelo."

"Every spy is accountable to someone even if that person is part of a group. So who are you accountable to? Who are you protecting?"

"The D.E.A."

Tate punches Chelo in the stomach.

"Give me the truth man! I don't need the D.E.A. bullshit. I have worked for the organization, you have to report to someone. Come on!"

That blow strikes Chelo hard. He coughs up blood as a result. Alberto Gomez looks at him as if to say: *don't waste my time. I did not fly in from China to be lied to.*

"Who was with you when you were captured?"

At this point, the *Dragons* are still unaware that Rude Buay has escaped death once again and is well alive and that he was with Chelo before being captured.

"No one. Why don't you ask Sal? He is standing right across from you."

Responds Chelo very calmly.

"Where are the rest of your guys?"

Questions Tate.

"I am not my brother's keeper. I work for the Drug Enforcement Agency."

Responds Chelo.

"Where is your satellite located?"

Asks Tate.

"That's a D.E.A. business."

Responds Chelo.

That feels like a slap on the face, to Miles Tate. He realizes that he is not going to get anything out of Chelo. Alberto Gomez and Salvador are all of the same opinions.

"How would you like to work for us?"

Interjects Alberto Gomez.

Chelo doesn't answer.

Alberto Gomez presents an attaché case filled with stacks of crisp U.S. One Hundred Dollar Bills.

Chelo looks them over.

"We'll pay you well. You sure know how to keep secrets."

Says Alberto Gomez.

"No thank you."

Responds Chelo.

"Give him a day or two to think about it. In the meantime prepare the gallows to hang his ...."

Says Alberto Gomez.

Tate ceases his questioning.

Salvador removes Chelo from the room. He puts him inside his pickup truck and escorts him back to the *small house* where he is kept under confinement.

25

While Rude Buay drives through the neighborhood looking for the missing Chelo his phone rings. It's his boss Ortiz on the other end. Rude Buay looks at the number on the caller ID and delays answering the call. After several rings, he accepts the call.

"Bascombe this is Ortiz. Would you like me to call you back?"

Asks Michael Ortiz.

"We can talk now."

Says Rude Buay.

Ortiz feels it in his agent's voice.

"You don't sound too…"

"Chelo is missing. Possibly captured!"

Informs Rude Buay,

"You are kidding me. Without him, we are dead in the water. Was it the *Dragons*?"

"Most likely! They have not claimed responsibility yet but…"

"Bascombe I told you, you've gotten in way too deep. Without him, it's over. Your entire team of agents could be wiped out at an instant. If you don't know where they are, it's like walking through a minefield. You need him to monitor those bastards especially at the border."

"That I know very well,"

Responds Rude Buay.

"I'm aware that Hudson recently joined you. She could have told me what her objective was instead of saying she wanted some time off."

States Ortiz.

'Really? Boss, I am not up on what Hudson does …"

Says Rude Buay.

"My suggestion is that you tell your team you are packing up and, return to Miami where at least it's not so bad and we have more control."

Says Ortiz.

"No thanks. I am not a quitter. There isn't a quitting cell in my makeup. I will fight them in the desert, I will fight them in the mountains, I will fight them in the tunnels, I will fight them amongst the cactus, I will fight them at the border, I will fight them in the air, and on the water … I will fight them everywhere. I am not giving in. All it takes for evil to prevail is a bunch of men with no backbone."

Declares Rude Buay.

"You are putting the lives of your teammates at risk, Bascombe. Maybe you should ask yourself the question. Why are we in Mexico? Additionally, what does the U.S. have to gain? They are our neighbors, not our friends. They bring us more harm than good. Why don't they sell it to their people? Their governmental views are opposed to ours. It is time to get out."

Says Ortiz.

"I hear you, boss. I am not going to quit so they can feel they have won. Plus, the man who saved my life from the gallows has probably been captured. And if there is even the remotest possibility that he is alive, then, I've got a job to do, and that is to find him. Quitting is not an option. *When the dream is strong enough, the facts don't count.* I need your support. If I can't have it, that's okay, I will fight this war alone till the end. I may lose some battles but I will not lose this war."

States Rude Buay.

"This is not the Winston Churchill era, Bascombe. He had Britain behind him. What do you have? Plus Chelo's understudy Bruce is very wet behind the ears."
Says Ortiz.
Rude Buay continues,
"Until one is committed, there is hesitancy, the chance to draw back, always ineffectiveness. Concerning all acts of initiative (or creation), there is only one truth, the ignorance of which kills many ideas and splendid plans, that the moment one definitely commits oneself, then Providence moves too.
All sorts of things occur to help one that would otherwise never have occurred. A whole stream of events issues from the decision, raising in one's favor all manner of incidents and meetings and material assistance: which no man would have believed would have come his way.
Whatever you think you can do or believe you can do begin it. Action has magic, grace, and power in it.' So said Goethe,"
Quotes Rude Buay.
Ortiz removes the phone receiver from his ear and stares at it, thinking Rude Buay has got to be crazy. He is fighting a Mexican war as long as the river Nile. Not only is he shorthanded but he's fighting with two injured hands.
"Hello,"
Says Rude Buay.

There is no answer coming from Ortiz on the other end of the phone. So Rude Buay hangs up on his end. After digesting the interlude between him and Ortiz, he reaches over on the front passenger seat. There sits the package with the pair of moccasins which he purchased for Chelo. He opens it and retrieves the shoe box. Rude Buay stares at the pair of moccasins.

"Requesting D.E.A. presence at an abandoned warehouse in Nogales just outside the Mexican border and across from Independence Street. Officer down! I repeat! One Border Patrol Officer down …!"

It is the voice of Bruce Chavez, Chelo's Mexican understudy.

Rude Buay makes a U-Turn in his jeep and heads speedily in that direction.

26

Rude Buay approaches the warehouse where the eighteen-wheelers were first seen. He had thought about using the tunnel but changes his mind and opts for the local street instead. In less than fifteen minutes he's at the border into Nogales. Moments later he pulls up at the warehouse once used as a clothing depot.

Flashing ambulance lights welcomes him along with busy medics surrounding the corpse of a uniformed border patrol officer.

Immediately after Rude Buay arrives on the scene, Mildred Simms, Richard Baptiste, Walter Banks, and Heidi Hudson pull up. They jump out of their jeeps and join in the investigation.

According to the eyewitness report of an elderly Mexican man:

Several cars were in line at the U.S. border crossing. Border patrol officers after detaining several Mexican motorists proceeded to search their vehicles. While rummaging through their cars, several teens arriving on foot from Nogales, Mexico emerged at the border crossing. In a confrontation, they demanded the release of those arrested. These kids armed to the max carrying AK47s opened fire on investigating border patrol officers as well as border workers.

When it all ended not only were several border patrols killed but the kids attempted to takeover border operations there in Nogales.

It was right about then that agent Rude Buay arrived on the scene.

The leader of the pack, a feisty Mexican kid, of dwarf stature and adorned in a bandanna. Yells out:

"We are the young "Dragons" and we are in control."

Rude Buay looking at him from a distance in his jeep says to himself:

"A minor is in control, he's got to be kidding. He could still be wetting his bed."

But looking at the waving AK47 in the kid's hands and the army of kids rallying for his support, the agent realizes that this is serious business. Plus there were no border patrols in sight except for those dead bodies lying around.

So Rude Buay decides to negotiate after summoning his backup of agents.

"Hey Kid! My name is agent Bascombe, D.E.A. You are indeed a tough kid. But whoever set you up to this is such a weakling, a coward. They should have done these acts themselves. You have no doubt so much potential and all your life ahead of you. Whoever set you up to this has nothing to live for…"

Interrupting the kid responds,

"Your name is not Bascombe, it's Rude Buay … aka Rude Boy. We don't need a sermon because we are not in church and today isn't Sunday. Plus, I dislike Sunday school. You are the man with the scorpion tattoo and causing a lot of trouble at our borders. You think this is Jamaica…! You've killed Johnny *Too Bad*, David Lee, Ian Baynes, Axel James, Desmond Scott, Jose Mendez, and Ricardo Herrera. You are not going to do the same for me!

The kid shoots off a round at Rude Buay. It misses.

"Look! Behind you coming through those hills are 10 eighteen-wheelers. We want their safe passage through this border which has for too long been like an iron wall to us Mexicans. When we feel they are safe we might be willing to discuss our plan B. I won't miss the next time around."

"What's inside of those trucks?"

Asks Rude Buay.

"None of your business!"

"Kid. Ever since 9/11, any vehicle entering the U.S. has to be checked. If I allow your trucks though, as an agent I would not be doing my job and could cause harm to many Americans."

The kid shoots at Rude Buay. Again he misses. The agent dodges out of the two rounds.

"That was just a warning. I want what I say, and I get what I want."

Says the kid.

"You are spoiled! What do your friends think? Are they in with you on this?"

Asks Rude Buay who would not let up off his aimed rifle at the kid.

"We don't have to listen to you. Look around you. The trucks are coming."

Says the kid.

Rude Buay peripherally sees another group of kids forming a circle around him.

"The choice is yours! In a minute over 30 bullets could be penetrating your body. Only one of mine… Do you want war or do you want peace?"

Yells the kid.

"Okay. I will let the trucks through, but one at a time."

Says Rude Buay,

The kid radios,

"Come on through, only one by one!"

Before the trucks could descend across the border, two jeeps emerge racing alongside them and raining tear gas onto the border compound.

Rude Buay grabs his mask and protects himself. Many stray bullets scatter from wielding AK47s, the experienced agents in both jeeps are unscathed. Caught up in the tear gas deposit the kids fall to the ground. The eighteen-wheelers are stalled in their tracks. Mildred Simms, Richard Baptiste, Walter Banks, and Heidi Hudson emerge from their vehicles. Along with agent Rude Buay, they pounce on the gassed kids, confiscating their weapons.

Moments later not only is the border reopened and manned by replaced border patrols, who are flown in, but 30 kids are arrested and detained along with 10 tractor-trailer drivers.

After a search of the eighteen-wheelers over 300,000 pounds of methamphetamine is seized along with 100,000 kilos of uncut cocaine.

27

fter this seizure, it became official news that not only was agent Rude Buay alive but that his team of agents was conducting U.S. D.E.A. duties in Mexico at the U.S border. Alberto Gomez now knew for sure that someone was covering Rude Buay when he was sent to the gallows or the men trusted to hang him, set him free, instead. So he put out a countrywide search in Mexico to have Rude Buay once again captured; so he could pull the trigger and take agent Rude Buay's life for good if he refused to team up. Rude Buay quickly learned of the Drug Czar's objective by signs placed on telephone poles. Hence, not only was he in pursuit of Rude Buay; for the possible kill, but Rude Buay was also in pursuit of him; and his entire team for *Operation Clean Sweep*.

It wasn't long after that, Bruce also discovered Alberto Gomez's plot, by tapping into a hotel phone line during his conference call with Salvador, Shelly Hall, Denise Gomez, Miles Tate, Marcus Ranks, Sammy Chin, and the remaining young *Dragons*. Bruce tipped off by an informant at the hotel was granted brief access to that Hotel's phone communication system. The informant made his side money that way.

Rude Buay, meanwhile, knew that no matter the many "what ifs" that surrounded Chelo's possibility of being still alive, he had to try his best to search and rescue him out of the grasp of the *Dragon Drug Cartel*. Rude Buay now waits outside his car at a local multicolored pottery shop in Nogales. He was informed by Bruce that Alberto Gomez, Denise and Shelly Hall frequented that block to shop and dine the *delicioso* local cuisine, known to awaken one's taste buds.

ONCE AGAIN THE VOICE of Bruce Chavez transmits through the D.E.A. radio circuit.

"Requesting D.E.A. presence at a food warehouse in Campillo and Belto Juarez. Two agents down."

There was no information on exactly who the fallen agents were. So, Rude Buay takes off in that direction. As do Banks and Heidi Hudson. Mildred Simms and Richard Baptiste also respond to the call. Three identical jeeps are now racing through Nogales, in Sonora, Mexico. Rude Buay's jeep is first to arrive at the scene, followed by Bank's jeep and then Mildred's. It's a bloody scene as two American agents lie on the street bathed in their blood and killed execution-style.

Rude Buay jumps out of his vehicle with his hands still bandaged. Walter Banks and Heidi Hudson using latex gloves gather information on the deceased agents by searching through their pockets and wallets.

"He is one of ours!"

Yells Hudson after viewing the first agent's ID. She views the second ID now handed to her by Walter Banks. Mildred Simms and Richard Baptiste yellow tape the area as they keep their eyes open for perpetrators.

Removing her gloves Hudson says,

"Both U.S. agents IDs are from New Mexico."

"What are they doing here by themselves? They should have known better than to be operating independently."

Says Rude Buay.

"What if Ortiz sent these men in to derail our progress? Heck, I wouldn't put it past him."

Says Hudson.

"Really?"

Asks Mildred.

"He is up for a promotion and needs people on his side."

Informs Rude Buay.

"Anything he can do to rank up, huh?"

Says Richard.

Rude Buay then calls in the Mexican *Policia*.

"Let's get out of here!"

Says Rude Buay.

As they get inside their vehicles and depart, Rude Buay senses being followed. His instincts are right on target as bullets instantly ring out raining on top of their vehicles.

BEFORE THE TWO AGENTS were gunned down. Both agents showed up at the warehouse: The purpose was for striking a deal with Denise Gomez and Shelly Hall for the purchase of 200 pounds of methamphetamine. The two men claimed they were from Los Angeles, California and were unable to acquire the product in the big city.

A drought had emerged in LA since those eighteen-wheelers were seized; loaded with narcotics, and bound for San Diego.

Conversely, those two agents from New Mexico were sent in by Michael Ortiz and Al Cortez. The latter was the head D.E.A. in New Mexico and wanted to help win support for Ortiz (to be known for) fighting the *Dragons* in Mexico. Both Special Agents were aware and concluded that Rude Buay and his team were taking the matter in Mexico into their own hands. More so, most Americans were now more tuned into what went on in Mexico and the drug trade because of the huge amounts of killings that ensued. They wanted to make sure their borders were intact and protection beefed up against the Mexicans. In a nutshell the reason for Ortiz's involvement; he woke up smelling the coffee and was now looking for shoulders that he could lean on. So he reached out to his ally, Cortez, in New Mexico.

As those two agents from New Mexico, posing as Drug Lords were led to the van loaded with drugs. They then returned to their car to hand over the attaché case filled with cash and collect the van's keys from the drug dealers. They had planned on one agent driving the vehicle to LA while the other followed in their car bearing California tags. Denise Gomez and Shelly Hall became suspicious. They wasted no time and snuffed them out with multiple rounds.

When Rude Buay and his team arrived, Shelly Hall and Denise Gomez were immediately interrupted as they attempted to reclaim possession of the 200 pounds of Meth aboard that van. Rude Buay and his team had passed the parked van and the car up the street not too far from where the two agents were gunned down.

They searched the van and not only was it loaded with meth but evidence indicated there could have been a chase of the two agents before they were shot and killed.

WITH THE DARK COLORED JEEP pursuing Rude Buay and his agents, the street race continued from Campillo onto Avenue Alvaro Obregon. Gaining some advantage and way ahead Rude Buay and his team pull off the road and into a secluded rest stop. The pursuing jeep continued and passed the rest area along the Avenue at high speed.
Moments later the three agent vehicles merged onto the Avenue in pursuit of the dark-colored jeep and its unknown occupants.

28

The three jeeps continue along the Avenue, moving at high speed to catch up to Shelly Hall and Denise Gomez's who's inside that vehicle. Inside the lead jeep is agent Rude Buay, followed by Walter Banks and behind Banks is Mildred Simms. Meanwhile, Shelly Hall and Denise Gomez are still oblivious that they are being followed by these D.E.A. agents. In their mindset they have no idea that who they are in pursuit of, are now their followers. Finally, it dawns on them that the agents took a detour. So instead of continuing on the Avenue they too take a detour through the hillside. They embark on a downgrade. As their vehicle makes its descent Rude Buay still in pursuit spots it.

Rude Buay radios Banks' and Simms' vehicle.

"That car is about a mile away going through the hills, step on it!"

Says Rude Buay.

"We are right on your tail, Rude Buay,"

Says Banks.

"We are covering you, Banks,"

Says Mildred.

Richard Baptiste, the Commissioner concurs.

The three agent's vehicles are now gaining ground on Denise Gomez's and Shelly Hall's vehicles.

Shelly Hall looks in her rearview mirror and discovers they are being followed closely. How she wished the table had turned right about then. The winding treacherous hills and valleys beckon along with this now desolate two-lane highway. Shelly Hall speeds up but right about that time Rude Buay's jeep is speedily catching up to hers.

The agents arm themselves in preparation for an imminent showdown with the two women. Rude Buay with one arm on the steering wheel and the other holding on to that rifle he has grown so accustomed to. The passenger window in his jeep is now rolled down as he places the barrel of his rifle on that door so it protrudes outside and points towards the vehicle ahead.

Banks' jeep is on Rude Buay's vehicle's tail. Heidi Hudson sitting in the passenger seat equips herself with her loaded semi-automatic. At this point, Hudson relives those taunting memories she suffered under the hands of oppression by Shelly Hall and Denise Gomez. Banks looking across at Hudson knows she is focused and ready for battle.

Inside Mildred Simms' vehicle, which tails Banks', is Baptiste the Jamaican Police Commissioner. He is armed with a semi-automatic weapon. Mildred maintains command of the road and is also armed with the same type of weapon. Baptiste could sense the tension but unfortunately not the extent of Mildred's vendetta against the two *femme Fatales*. He rolls down the window and cues his gun in the same manner as Rude Buay's, as if by design.

At the same time, Shelly Hall's vehicle picks up speed. Her gun sits between her seat and the passenger seat. Denise occupying that passenger seat prepares for battle with her gun in hand. The agent's vehicles also pick up the pace.

Rude Buay get a few shots off. Unfortunately, nothing connects. Denise responds with a few of her own. Same result, *Zilch, Nada*, Nothing Connects!

Rude Buay's vehicle is now so close it's almost rear-ending Shelly Hall's. The road opens up providing a shoulder. Rude Buay speeds up and takes it. He is poised to get a good shot off at Shelly Hall. Shelly Hall drives out of the shot which sails into space.

Shelly Hall's vehicle is now in full view to agent Banks and Hudson as Rude Buay tries to make up for that missed opportunity to shoot Shelly Hall.

Heidi Hudson blasts several rounds at the two women. While Rude Buay and Shelly Hall jockey for position, Hudson tries passing on the other side and is almost at even keel with Denise's raised gun. Shelly Hall speeds up oblivious to the fact that she has derailed Rude Buay's focused gun on her. Now she drives leaving room on the left. Rude Buay tries positioning parallel with her vehicle so he can get a great aim at Shelly Hall. Instead, Shelly Hall tries forcing his jeep into the gutter.

Hudson's round of bullets connects with the two rear tires on Shelly Hall's vehicle and punctures both tires. Shelly Hall's car is slowed as it wobbles. Hudson manages to get another round-off, which blows out the rear windscreen.

In the meantime, a shot from Hudson's gun strikes Denise Gomez. Rude Buay also gets a shot off which hits Shelly Hall. Not only is Shelly Hall hit, but she also loses control of the vehicle. As a result, her vehicle nosedives over the steep embankment, rolling several times. It stops after crashing into a huge tree.

The agents get out of their vehicles and assess the damage from the roadway up above. From their vantage point, the two doors are ajar on this totaled vehicle. Mildred Simms and Heidi Hudson finish it off with several rounds, setting it ablaze. The agents depart I haste.

29

R ude Buay and his agents are combing the city of Nogales, Mexico. They are looking for any lead in finding Chelo.

"Requesting D.E.A. presence at the Nogales, Arizona border! Five border patrol officers down. They are at the scene where two illegal trailers are trying to cross into the U.S. from Mexico. They could be loaded with narcotics." The voice of Bruce echoes over the radios inside the three jeeps manned by the D.E.A. agents. Bruce conducts his survey from the hills of Nogales,

Mexico in a small house overlooking the U.S. border with Mexico.

Rude Buay, Walter Banks, Heidi Hudson, Mildred Simms, and Richard Baptiste take off towards the crime scene. Upon arrival they catch one of the drivers who later revealed his name as Javier, searching through the pockets of one of the fallen border patrol officers. The other driver waited inside the cab of his eighteen-wheeler in anticipation of getting the go-ahead from Javier. That decision to drive his trailer across the U.S. border was halted by the agent's presence.

During their investigation, the agents discover three border patrol vehicles parked on the street: Vehicles which probably served as impediments to the trailer's crossing into the U.S. Next to those means of transportation, are three dead officers and two on the pavement outside the border compound.

Upon the arrival of the agents, Javier and the other driver did not surrender but fired several rounds at them. The agents before they could get a shot off, they heard gunshots from both the men:

"Click! Click!

Those were the sound coming from the two drug smugglers guns. The two men try fleeing the scene back into Mexico but are caught by the agents and placed in handcuffs.

Rude Buay questions Javier about his involvement sensing that he was the ring leader. Rude Buay asks him what he was looking for in the officer's pocket. Javier tells the agent he was looking for keys. He also tells the agent that he is from Nogales in Sedona, Mexico. He further discloses that he has two daughters, 10 and 11. Also, Javier says that his wife Nora was killed in a drive-by shooting several months prior leaving him a widower. The other driver only reveals that his name is Jesus when asked by Rude Buay. Besides, he doesn't say very much. Rude Buay asks Javier for his two daughter's pictures. The smuggler has none to present, neither does he have any photos of his deceased wife.

Rude Buay asks him why he took the lives of the Border Patrol Officers. Javier said bluntly:

"They stood in our way. They block the street, asking what's inside the truck. I said none of your ... business! They shoot ... first. I had to defend."

Rude Buay wants to believe him but Javier doesn't look him in the eye.

Meanwhile, the accompanying D.E.A. agents discover large quantities of narcotics inside both trailers. Rude Buay asks the men why they were smuggling drugs into the U.S., to whom, and who they were working for? Javier tells Rude Buay they were paid to drive the trailers from Nogales to El Paso because there was trouble at the El Paso border. There in El Paso, they would transfer the trailers and drive back to Mexico. Javier discloses that they were hired by the *Dragon Drug Cartel*. When asked who in the organization they reported directly to. Javier informs they reported directly to Salvador.

Rude Buay then questions Javier about Salvador's whereabouts. Javier says he couldn't say, he didn't want to be any snitch, or else the *Dragons* would kill him by hanging him from a pole.

After pressuring Javier further to disclose Sal's whereabouts Javier attains a comfort level with agent Rude Buay. So, Javier tells Rude Buay that Salvador stays at the Cactus Motel in Nogales.

Rude Buay feels that he has gotten the info he wants. Before departing with the other DEA agents additional border officers show up at the border. They take Javier and Jesus into custody and charge them with murder and drug smuggling.

Rude Bauy says to his other agents, departing.

"Let's get ... out of here!"

30

Upon arriving at the *Cactus Motel*, the huge cactus plants on the premises very much compliment the signage. The hotel parking lot at mid-afternoon is almost empty. Many guests are checking in and out.

Javier had lied so much when questioned by Rude Buay, he felt this could be nothing but a hoax. Even so, he goes inside the motel lobby. Walking up to the counter Rude Buay tells the receptionist he is a U.S. D.E.A. and that he is looking for Salvador.

"He no here,"

The middle-aged woman says nervously.

"Where is he now?"

Asks Rude Buay.

"Nobody here right now. New people check-in."

Replies the woman.

Looking out at the almost empty parking lot Rude Buay asks,

"Did he check out? I don't see his pickup truck. What color was it again?"

Rude Buay points his rifle towards the woman's head.

"Green!"

Says the woman.

"Where's his room?

The agent asks.

"He left, *señor*."

She responds.

"Is he coming back?"

Rude Buay asks,

"I don't know. No speak English!"

Rude Buay get the message. She knows but would not divulge. So Rude Buay waits along with his agents. While they wait for Sal to show up, breaking news airs over a Jamaican TV station and is transmitted through to the agent's vehicles:

"*Two Jamaican Police Officers were gunned down earlier this morning by drug dealers in Tivoli Gardens using weapons from the Fast & Furious program. It was said that police was informed about an alleged drug deal of Methamphetamine.*

One source said: When police arrived on the scene, members of the Dragon Drug Cartel, aligned with Jamaican Drug Lord Marcus Ranks, prowled on the two officers. Their arsenal instantly outmatched that of the police. The officers died suddenly.

Meanwhile, Methamphetamine in large quantity continues to pour into Tivoli Gardens, Port Antonio and Kingston. It was also claimed that many teens who have used the drug in the past continue to suffer from the slowness of both their brain and body."

States the reporter.

Moments later vehicles started pulling into the driveway sporadically. The guests continue to check-in. There is no sign of Salvador. The other agents look at Rude Buay as if they weren't sure this motel raid is going to go down.

Finally, the green pickup pulls into the parking lot. Sal appears, dressed in skinny jeans along with with a rolled-up sleeves white shirt unbuttoned at the top, a straw hat and a pair of black and white alligator boots. Sal prepares to enter his room on the hotel's ground level.

Rude Buay steps out of his jeep armed with a gun in hand. He is covered by Walter Banks, Heidi Hudson,

Mildred Simms, and Richard Baptiste. As soon as Sal turns the key inside the door lock and pushes it open, Rude Buay in pursuit yells out:

"Don't move Sal, U.S. Drug Enforcement Agents!"

Sal is alerted and tries closing the door on them. Instead, Sal abruptly aborts his entry to make his getaway. Rude Buay pushes him inside using the barrel portion of his rifle before Sal can get a shot off.

Sal's room is now filled with DEA agents. The atmosphere looks like an extended stay by its occupant Sal, instead of a weekend getaway. The odor says he's been staying there for a while; his BO and the room have blended.

Sal remains crouched on the floor with agents guns pointed at him. Rude Buay moves pass Sal's Meth lab which is set up inside a cubicle. He couldn't help but notice the test tubes inside this well-structured laboratory.

Additionally, he hears a moaning in the other room. He investigates.

Rude Buay's attention is drawn to a man tied up on a chair with his back turned. Rude Buay pushes the chair around with his feet. Surprisingly enough it is Chelo, tied up on that chair with multiple nylon ropes. Additionally, Chelo's right thumb and index fingers are bandaged and bloodied, indicating that some of his fingernails have already been removed. Rude Buay reminisces about the nail removal process he underwent at the hands of the dragons. He glances at his hands still bandaged. Even so, he senses difficulty untying the nylon ropes. So he summons Heidi Hudson:

Hudson darts into the room. She pulls out a switchblade from inside her boots under her jeans. She cuts the ropes which bind Chelo. The battered Chelo gets up from the chair somewhat lethargic and discombobulated. Hudson helps him out to the living room.

"Let's move it!"

Commands Rude Buay.

They get ready to leave. Salvador is still on the floor face down. He tries to get up in retaliation. Even so, he notices three guns are pointed at him. His shirt is now unbuttoned. Visible on his body are multiple second-degree burns. Rude Buay senses that their origin comes as a result of Sal's involvement in Methamphetamine preparation.

Rude Buay asks Salvador,

"Where is Alberto Gomez?"

Sal doesn't reply.

"Sal, where is your boss Alberto Gomez?"

Once again Sal doesn't respond.

Rude Buay shoots Sal in his right leg.

Still, Sal does not inform Rude Buay regarding his boss' whereabouts. So he shoots Sal a second time this time in the other leg.

In pain, Sal responds.

"Jamaica!"

Rude Buay pumps two more rounds inside Sal's body putting him out of his misery. The agents depart from the motel room.

While the agents went up to Salvador's room. The woman attendant at the front desk had called some of Sal's contacts alerting them that D.E.A. agents were after Sal and had headed over to his motel room.

As the agents arrive at the front parking lot of the *Cactus Motel*, they are greeted by a group of armed men. The men of Mexican descent are in a huddle waving machetes and cutlasses towards the D.E.A. agents. One of the men says to the leader of the pack:

"Let's chop them … up."

Rude Buay hears and proceeds towards them with his rifle in hand. "Let's chop Rude Buay up to pieces."

Echoes the leader of the pack,

"I will take them on solo."

Says Rude Buay to his agents.

"You are crazy, *mon*! You don't know who you are dealing with."

Says Banks to Rude Buay.

"I wouldn't stop him if he thinks he can avoid getting chopped up by these Mexicans."

Says Baptiste.

"Get them Rude Buay!"

Says Heidi and Mildred in touché fashion.

"That's okay. Their asses are mine."

Rude Buay thinks about taking them on with some sweeping rounds but at the same time the leader of the pack Julio, holding on to an extended *one seamed cutlass* invitingly signals Rude Buay into a duel. Rude Buay never passes up a challenge and he was not about to pass this one up. So he advances towards Julio in confrontation. Julio separates himself from the rest of the crowd for leverage. He sucks Rude Buay into the duel.

To the amazement of the other D.E.A. agents, Rude Buay takes on Julio one on one with his rifle in hand. They begin sparring at each other. Julio's posse is now transformed into spectators as well as the other agents. All onlookers were now transfixed as the cutlass was swung at Rude Buay on many occasions. Rude Buay threw a few flying kicks at Julio for a while, none of which connect.

Finally, a kick from Rude Buay catches Julio in his stomach area. Julio tries to catch his breath. His cutlass soars and hits the pavement "CLING! CLANG!" as the kick from Rude Buay catches him unexpectedly. Rude Buay tosses his rifle in the direction of the agents and goes at Julio barehanded.

Julio ingeniously recovers his cutlass and swings at Rude Buay. Mildred and Hudson tremble like a leaf. Unfortunately, the swing from Julio misses Rude Buay.

Julio swings at him again. This time Mildred has her finger on the trigger ready to blast Julio.

Rude Buay does a 360 and plants a flying kick in Julio's neck area. Julio spins around and falls to the ground, in pain. Julio struggles to get up and falls back to the ground. He clenches tightly to his neck. Julio's posse comes charging at Rude Buay with cutlasses and machetes.

Rude Buay retrieves his rifle and blasts the entire lot of Julio's posse.

Rude Buay and the DEA agents re-board their vehicles and depart forthwith.

Meanwhile, the woman attendant at the reception office takes stock of the bloodbath from behind the hotel lobby blinds.

31

The next morning the agents arrive in Montego Bay Jamaica on the heels of Dr. Tamara Ross who has just reported for duty at the Port Antonio General Hospital. Dr. Ross was immediately put in charge of over a dozen patients, mostly teens, suffering from Methamphetamine overdose.

After exiting the airport terminal, the agents were met and greeted by a *Distinguished Gentleman*. He is dressed in white clothing and also sports a well-manicured beard.

"Mr. Rude Buay, it's good to see you again. If you survived the Villa, Tivoli Gardens, Shanghai, and Nogales, you can survive this. Although I must inform you that the man you will come up against Marcus Ranks, is more dangerous than Axel James, Frankie O'Neal, Ian Baynes, Ricardo Herrera and Johnny *Too Bad*. His skills outmatch theirs. Plus, he could very shortly be joined by Alberto Gomez. Here are the keys and directions. It is filled with gas. It has only been driven once. Your toys from the *Fast & Furious* program are in the trunk. You are going to need them."

"Thanks, but I love my rifle. I've grown accustomed to it. Plus..."

Says Rude Buay.

The other agents look on at the exchange between the two men.

"Agent Rude Buay, you must match your firepower to the new weapons used by the *Dragon Drug Cartel* or you and your team would be outmatched by Marcus Ranks in Kingston. You must conquer your comfort zone. This is the age of the *fast and furious*. Your country needs you."

The *Distinguished Gentleman* mounts his white horse and departs.

Rude Buay and his agents board the extended SUV and head speedily for Kingston.

The following morning the agents arrive in Kingston. Walter Banks questions if they should divide to conquer. Rude Buay, on the other hand, feels that unity is strength. He feels like they are about to bring in Marcus Ranks. With him leading the quest, accompanied by Banks, Simms, Baptiste, Hudson, and Chelo, Rude Buay feels whoever they came up against at this point had no chance.

As they drive through the busy streets of Kingston, a youth no more than seventeen crosses the street amid the traffic. Not only do many motorists, including Rude Buay, apply brakes but honk their horns. The retard does not heed any warning. Luckily he escapes being run over. He crosses the street and joins a weed-smoking huddle across the street. Hudson in the rear of the SUV shakes her head in dismay.

Later they pull up at *The Cave*. This hole in the wall was first on the list received from the *Distinguished Gentleman*. This was known as a possible hang out spot for Marcus Ranks.

The SUV pulls up and parks in-front of *The Cave*. Rude Buay sees a youth leaving the spot.

"Hey youth man! You saw Marcus Ranks lately?"

Asks Rude Buay.

"I don't talk to no police."

Says the youth.

"What you have against us?"

Asks Hudson.

"Nothing, I mind my own business. He just left an hour ago. Try the shooting range."

Rude Buay sticks a hundred dollar bill inside the youth's hand. They take off hurriedly through Kingston.

32

The agents pull up in front of the shooting range nestled in a backlot of a slum in Kingston. They quickly exit the SUV. Rude Buay, Banks, and Hudson barges in while the others cover. Inside a group of shooters hone their skills. They were later identified as Marcus Ranks' posse. These shooters are all hitting their targets as they are all going for the shooting target's head.

Rude Buay, Walter Banks and Heidi Hudson all *sign up* as guests to investigate the posse.

Unfortunately by the time the D.E.A. agents are finished, fitted and set to begin their shooting workout, the posse had already returned their weapons and made their exit through the back parking lot.

The agents return the following day. Except for this time they show up an hour earlier. Rude Buay, Walter Banks and Heidi Hudson are now involved in their shooting exercise. They are accompanied by Chelo undergoing an intense training session directed by agent Rude Buay. Chelo very early on is very much on target hitting the bulls-eye. His shots land in the head and stomach regions successively. The agents applaud his efforts, especially Walter Banks with an extended version.

Marcus Ranks still doesn't show up. The agents return the gear and head out. On their way to the parking lot, Marcus Rank's posse comes barging in. This time Rude Buay approaches them with his drawn *F & F* gun as soon as they exit their cars.

"Hold it right there! Drug Enforcement Agents!" Announces Rude Buay.

Before the posse of four men and two women could arm themselves, they find themselves surrounded by all six D.E.A. agents armed with *F and F* program weapons.

The other agents cover while Rude Buay, Banks and Hudson search their vehicles. The agents discover inside the trunks several pounds of Meth and kilos of cocaine. Baptiste accommodates several pairs of handcuffs retrieved from inside the rear of the SUV.

Moments later, the posse is sitting on the sidewalk in handcuffs and being questioned by Rude Buay. The agent continues:

"I understand you are affiliated with the 'Wanted Marcus Ranks.' Not only that, but you were also caught in possession of illegal drugs as well as illegal firearms. Crimes like these could keep you in a Jamaican prison for a serious time. You can get those times reduced substantially however if you choose to cooperate by leading us to Marcus Ranks."

One of the women says,

"We don't know any Marcus Ranks!"

"Yes, you do Megan Holt."

Says the Commissioner looking at her straight on,

The Commissioner continues after Megan Holt looks away:

"Our records indicate that you provided Officer Bascombe with a constant supply of Methamphetamine. That drug which not only caused the death of his daughter Glenda but also caused the officer to take his own life. That supply was traced to Meth prepared by the *Dragons* and sold in Jamaica by you along with Marcus Ranks as the middle man."

"How much time is going to be knocked off of this deal?"

Asks the other woman.

All eyes are now on Rude Buay.

The woman continues,

"Because ..."

"Shut up bitch ..."

Says the leader of the pack, a midget, adorned in a black, gold and green tam, covering up his dreadlocks hairstyle.

The Commissioner remarks,

"We will be willing to negotiate on your behalf."

"Look for the ship *Marc I*. He docks at the pier at nights."

The rest of the posse looks at Megan Holt as if she was crazy to rattle on their boss.

Once again, the leader of that pack addresses,

"What makes you think these PIGS are going to help you get your time reduced?"

In the interim, the Commissioner calls in the Jamaican Police. They have just arrived on the scene. They quickly take the six members of Marcus Ranks' posse into custody.

33

The agents swarm the dock at Kingston later that night in search of Marcus Ranks. This stakeout by the agents results in a no show once again by Marcus Ranks.

The following morning agent Rude Buay receives a text message from Bruce still stationed in Mexico that the *Dragons* were meeting in South Beach, Miami. Attendees at that meeting are supposed to be Alberto Gomez, Miles Tate, Grace McCloud, Sammy Chin, and Marcus Ranks according to the text message. So the agents later board a plane bound for Miami.

IN SOUTH BEACH, MIAMI: Hip-Hop and Rap music reverberates from sidewalk bars, restaurants and night clubs on a busy evening. Some even entertain with House music and R & B from underneath their tents. Hot women, some of them attired in tight jeans, others in miniskirts and some in cheeky shorts parade the streets during the early evening hours. The men salivate, casting multiple double-takes.

Drug dealers and buyers conduct business managing to avoid Law Enforcement Officers, as they use their two-way radio feature on their cell phones to alert each other of danger zones. Street after street is crowded with pedestrians. The vibe is like that of a Memorial Day weekend in South Beach. Buses even avoid making stops along some of those pedestrian crowded streets. The sidewalks are roped off and barricaded, thus allowing a steady easy flow of pedestrians.

The nearby restaurants, bars, stores, and clubs are buzzing with activity. Never before has South Beach drawn such a crowd except on a Memorial Day weekend. Miami police walk the beat as a routine. The drug pushers and buyers cleverly escape their surveillance as narcotics trade hands.

Meanwhile, in a South Beach hotel suite, a meeting is in session: five members of the Dragon drug Cartel convene to save the depleting *Dragon Drug Cartel*. Some of the topics being discussed are:

1) Eliminating Rude Buay and his agents to allow free trade between Mexico and the rest of the world if he will not agree to sign onto the team.
2) Adding new members to the cartel.
3) Sabotaging the efforts of competing cartels in Mexico like the Sinaloa Cartel.

Alberto Gomez chairs the meeting. Additionally, he displays pictures on a TV monitor:

1. Several closed and out of business Nogales local banks.
2. Mexican drug smugglers reverting to making pottery and other handcraft products.
3. Border patrols surveying the drug tunnel operations between Mexico and Arizona.
4. The discontinued drug activity at many abandoned warehouses in Mexico.
5. Pictures of Rude Buay's duel with Julio as taken from the woman at the hotel's POV.
6. Pictures of Sal's corpse.
7. Pictures of Victor Crip's corpse.
8. Government workers in Arizona sealing up the manholes at the parking meters on Independence Street.
9. Eighteen-wheelers carry drugs across the U.S. border seized by border patrols.
10. The overturned car once occupied by Denise Gomez and Shelly Hall

At this point, Alberto Gomez turns off the monitor. He has seen enough. He is not the only one who is frustrated so do the other members of his team.

He articulates,

"Guys we need to act now not only to recapture those D.E.A. agents but to hold our cartel together. Let's not forget, we are *The Dragons*. We Rule! I will not let another Mexican cartel thrive on what we have put in place for so many years."

"How soon will a new Chemist be reinstated…?"

Asks Miles Tate.

"Same question."

Interrupts Marcus Ranks.

"We have many orders to fill in New England and neighboring cities."

Says Miles Tate.

"Miami is going to be dry after this weekend. Plus I can't keep my Cuban customers waiting much longer. Their patience is running thin."

Says Grace McCloud.

Before Sammy Chin can speak, Grace follows up by saying:

"It is the first time we have ever had a shortage of supply here in Miami. Pushers have doubled their prices for both Meth and Cocaine. We are in no position to compete with members of neither the Sunshine Cartel nor the Sinaloa … in this marketplace."

"If anyone has an extra supply of Meth let me know. I will have to smuggle it into China myself. Shipping it would take too long. Chu Ling's clients are waiting. Don't want to piss them off."

Says Sammy Chin,

"I have found a new Chemist, His name is Chico Rubio. The first mixes could be a little harsh until he gets seasoned. We'll just have to market our product anyway."

Says Alberto Gomez.

"What about possible recalls?"

Asks Sammy Chin.

"No recalls. I don't like that dirty word."

Says Alberto Gomez.

"That's a hard pill for Jamaicans to swallow."

Says Marcus Ranks.

He is not clearly understood. So he clarifies.

"Could we buy from another source until Chico Rubio gets a hang of this?"

"I would not endorse buying from the Sunshine or Sinaloa Cartel. They are part of what got us in this glut. If they had not tried sending so many eighteen-wheelers loaded with the product across the U.S. border we would not be in the glut we are in. Never rush the Americans. They get you all the time. Slow and steady wins the race. This meeting is adjourned. If anyone runs into Rude Buay, I have my gun loaded with bullets initialed RB."

Alberto Gomez exits and boards a waiting limousine. The others board individual taxis as they leave the South Beach hotel.

34

Rude Buay, Chelo, Banks, Heidi Hudson, Mildred Simms, and Richard Baptiste embark upon South Beach with a vengeance. Once again they pair up for battle with the *Dragon Drug Cartel*. Agent Rude Buay reunites with Chelo in the first car. Walter Banks and Heidi Hudson are in the second car and Mildred Simms and Richard Baptiste in the third.

The agent convoy moves through the streets of South Beach in a surveillance style. With many of the main boulevards blocked off with barricaded sidewalks, the agents take a detour using the open side streets. They pull up at the hotel where the *Dragons* had just wrapped their meeting. After parking their vehicles they barge inside armed to the maximum. A hotel employee but who is also an inside informant directs them to the executive suite.

Rude Buay knocks on the door, no one answers. Using his gun he blows out the lock. They enter. A few pens and scrap paper residue is evidence a meeting was in session. The delegation, on the other hand, is absent. The agents depart to the outside re-board their vehicles and head off through the streets of South Beach.

The streets, although only accessible to minimal vehicular traffic has become more traffic-laden than when the agents arrived on the strip. The gridlock traffic creates a bottleneck for South Beach exiting traffic. The agents are now caught up in that going-nowhere, very slowly, dilemma.

Rude Buay as if equipped with the eyes of a hawk spots the getaway SUV with Miles Tate in the driver's seat. He alerts his other agents via radio and pursues Miles Tate. Rude Buay's vehicle weaves in and out of traffic as he tries to catch up with Tate's. His other agents follow suit in tow.

Meanwhile, inside Tate's SUV, Tate with the use of his side mirrors sees the aggressively pursuant. Rude Buay's vehicle has now passed several cars and aligned itself three cars ahead making it the fourth car behind Tate's. Not only does Tate notice the pursuing Rude Buay, but he also notices, the other two cars accompanying Rude Buay. In an instant that vehicle careens around those three cars using the shoulder of the street and is now exactly behind Tate's SUV.

The pressure is now building on Tate's end as the only exit from Beach Street is the beach exit. The buses transporting passengers to and from South Beach have all clogged up the boulevards. Not only that, he knows that Rude Buay wants his head on a platter for deflecting and being a snitch. He also notices Chelo accompanying the agent and occupying the front seat. Two men who should have been dead are following him along with four other survivors.

Tate reaches for his gun as he opts to exit on the street leading towards the beach. The agents are right up behind him tailgating. Tate's vehicle is slowed by the sand on the beach, but more so, the vehicles of the agents in pursuit. The sedans finally split from the convoy and form a periphery around the SUV.

Tate jumps out and fires off a few rounds at the agents before making his plunge into the water. Not only do his rounds miss their target but Rude Buay is only a few feet away in pursuit. Tate tries to swim away into the deep but Rude Buay is about to have him cornered. The agent yells at Tate as he tries to dive:

"Tate there isn't anywhere to run to. I told you if you ever became a snitch we would go fishing. Even so, you are too big a *bait* for Jack Fish. Plus, they only thrive in the Caribbean, not in Miami. The sharks would be happy though. They are always drawn to human blood.

Tate tries to get a kick, aimed at Rude Buay. He misses. They have now squared off waist-deep in the water. Rude Buay throws a left jab and a right uppercut. Tate is hit by the jab to his face but as he ducks in the uppercut escapes him.

Rude Buay throws him a right jab which lands in his mouth causing him to spit out blood as a result.

Banks standing on the beach with the other agents, yells:

"Let me shoot the bastard. No need to get saturated with *his* blood! Nothing but a … traitor!"

The water rises as they are drawn in deeper by the tide. Rude Buay pushes Tate under and refuses to let up. Tate begins kicking for his existence. Yet, Rude Buay does not let him up. Tate drinks until he can drink no more. Rude Buay releases him to his death and returns to the beach. Before Tate's body submerges Chelo fires a round at the ex-agent. It connects to his head. Tate goes under.

As they get ready to re-board he gets a call from D.E.A. headquarters requesting his presence at the Miami harbor. The call is regarding a ship alleged to be loaded with narcotics. Without a chance to change out from the wet clothing, Rude Buay and his agents rush, to the Miami port accompanied by sirens and flashing lights.

35

The agents pull up in their BMW's at Miami Harbor. They notice the harbor saturated with multiple ships. With the use of binoculars, they try to determine the target ships carrying out the narcotics transfer. Rude Buay zooms out and locates their targets. He alerts the other agents.

The agents quickly board a speedboat heading in that direction. The speedboat takes off navigating its way through the crowded port, leaving an extended trail of white water behind it.

As they are nearing the ship which made the transfer, that ship raises its anchor and takes off. The other ship named *Marc 1* is about to do the same. Banks at the helm of their speedboat pulls up in front of the *Marc 1's* bow. The man lifting the anchor alerts the rest of the crew. Bullets from *Marc 1* begin to rain onto DEA the agent's speedboat. The agents manage to dodge out of those bullets. Before Richard Baptiste, now in command of the ship, abandons it he attaches a rope to *Marc 1* using a lasso.

Rude Buay and Walter Banks have already jumped aboard the suspected *Marc I*. Two men aboard the *Marc I* see the agents approaching and train their weapons on them. The sight of the agent's *F & F's* weapons has the two men with their backs up against the wall. Another man armed approaches from the hull. Rude Buay yells out:

"D.E.A.! Hands on your heads."

The three men comply with the agent's request.

"Where is Marcus Ranks?"

Asks Rude Buay.

"He is not here."

Says the last man to exit the hull of the ship dressed in a dreadlocks hairstyle.

"Where is he?"

Asks Rude Buay.

"No idea."

Says the man.

"You are under arrest for drug smuggling."

Says Rude Buay.

Banks, Hudson and Baptiste put handcuffs on the three men while Rude Buay and Chelo descend inside of the hull. Rude Buay and Chelo discover several bags of marijuana, over 500 pounds of methamphetamine and about 300 kilos of cocaine in addition to an assortment of weapons and U.S. currency.

On the outside, the *Marc 1* lifeboat's engine starts up. Helming it is Marcus Ranks who had previously emerged from under some tarpaulin on the other side of the *Marc 1*. He is about to make his getaway.

Inside the hull Rude Buay sees Ranks trying to make his getaway from through the porthole. Rude Buay takes off with Chelo. Passing through the deck Banks joins them. The three agents board the speedboat in pursuit of Marcus Ranks.

Meanwhile, Michael Ortiz is standing on the bridge across the way overlooking the harbor and watching the unfolding of events through a pair of binoculars. Rude Buay, Banks, and Chelo continue to go after Marcus Ranks at full speed.

Ranks sees them rapidly approaching and fires off a few quick rounds, tragically catching nothing, but air.

Banks is at the helm of the speed boat. Chelo is now on the phone with Ortiz talking about their next plan of attack on the *Dragons*. Rude Buay get a good aim at Ranks and blasts him. Marcus Ranks is hit in the chest.

He falls over into the lifeboat. His boat continues and crashes into a pillar upholding the bridge.

The agents return to the *Marc 1* and wrap up their narcotics seizure. They depart in the speedboat as Miami police now on the scene arrest the three drug smugglers and confiscate the seizure of narcotics.

36

The agents pull up in front of the club *Dynasty* dressed to the nines. Even so, Chelo is the only one not part of the group. They pull up outside and enter flashing their badges. Inside the club, it's a party as usual. The agents mingle. The vibe on the inside puts South Beach in the evening, on a whole other level. *Go Go Dancers* dance from inside huge glass cases. Hot babes saunter throughout the club. Surfer type males interact with these Hotties. Some are fortunate to get a number. On the other hand, the more passive men wait at the bar to make their approach. The agents survey and have a few drinks.

RICHARD BAPTISTE'S WIFE Christine calls. Richard answers.

"When are you coming home, Richard? I miss you!"

He tells her that the Miami situation has become very demanding. He also reminds her that he would be home on time for her birthday in two weeks.

Christine, after ending the conversation looks at the calendar hanging over the fridge, and then plops down on the couch and continues playing her game of Solitaire and enjoying a glass of Merlot.

AT THE CLUB Mildred approaches Richard and signals him to the dance floor. The DJ had just put on a dancehall tune. The DJ mixes it with a soca beat. Mildred goes wild putting Richard under severe pressure to keep up with her on the dance floor. She is now center stage with Richard. The other agents cheer them on. So do the heavily gathering party crowd.

The band gets ready to set up for their musical performance. Rude Buay signals time to leave. They head towards the backstage.

Behind the curtain is the new look Chelo, dressed in a sharp business suit, a tailored shirt with a smashing tie. On his feet, he wears the pair of moccasins which Rude

RUDE BUAY VOL. III

Buay bought him back in Mexico on the day he was captured by Salvador. It is a spit shine. This wardrobe upgrade gives him the look of a Cuban businessman, enhanced with a hat and a cigar.

Through the back exit door walks Grace McCloud. The *femme fatale* is carrying a duffel bag in her hand. Back there Chelo waits for solo but with a certain degree of confidence. McCloud presents the bag to Chelo. He opens it and inspects its contents. He is satisfied. Chelo hands over the attaché case to McCloud. To her, it is the right amount of cash for the 15 pounds of Methamphetamine and the 5 kilos of cocaine. The case is closed quickly and McCloud walks towards the exit door to the parking lot. Chelo picks up the bag of narcotics heading towards the stage.

Before McCloud could get to the door, Rude Buay, Walter, Heidi, Mildred, and Richard have her cornered.

"Hold it right there McCloud! D.E.A., nobody moves!" Chelo stays put to accommodate. The four agents pass him by and hold McCloud at gunpoint. McCloud calls them bluff and heads through the door, quickly dodging rounds of bullets, before boarding the waiting limousine.

They pursue and shoot up the trying to get away limousine. McCloud showing resilience opens the moon roof and fire off several rounds at the agents. The agents run out of bullets in their semi-automatic weapons as a result of the onslaught on the limo. McCloud is hit but continues to shoot back at the agents.

From underneath the table, Chelo speedily wheels out an open trunk filled with *F & F's*. Rude Buay, Walter, Heidi, Mildred and Richard once again return fire on McCloud and her limo driver, this time from the state of the art weapons. The limo gets demolished with McCloud and the chauffeur inside.

The agents depart while the patrons rush to the back parking lot.

37

As the agents leave the club and merge with the boulevard traffic. Rude Buay's phone rings. It's a familiar number as revealed by his caller ID. On the other end is his boss Michael Ortiz.

Rude Buay did you get them?"

Agent Ortiz asks.

"Yes. I did!"

Says Rude Buay.

"Both of them?"

Asks his boss.

"Yep!"

Says Rude Buay,

"McCloud and Chin?"

Asks Ortiz.

"Chin wasn't there."

Says Rude Buay.

"He followed McCloud to make the drop for Chelo and then he went to fill up at the gas station."

"Really? What is he driving?"

Asks Rude Buay.

"A Cadillac Escalade, ivory in color. Do not let him get away, Rude Buay,"

Says Ortiz.

Rude Buay is *gamed*.

The agents speed up.

Moments later Rude Buay notices the Escalade speedily moving in the direction to the club. He and his team make a U-Turn and follow that vehicle. As they close in, on it, he recognizes Sammy Chin under the driver's seat. The blue lights on his dash begin to flash and revolve. The other agents follow suit as he is now tailgating Chin's vehicle.

Chin would not let up. An intense chase ensues. Chin seems like he is about to make a getaway on the open roads. He continues to pursue Chin with his agents following in tow. The chase continues through the back roads of South Beach. Rude Buay is now close enough to the Escalade and gets a shot off at Chin. The bullet hits the front left fender of the vehicle. Chin begins to fight back with several rounds. Rude Buay and his agent begin to shoot up the Escalade with an onslaught of bullets. Chin is hit. As a result the SUV slams into a retaining wall. Rude Buay searches the SUV and discovers at least 50 pounds of Methamphetamine inside a duffel bag.

Rude Buay goes through Chin's wallet and discovers two hotel room keys and a check-in receipt billed to Gomez's credit card.

38

Rude Buay, cognizant of the fact that where there is smoke there is Alberto Gomez still at large. So he heads for the *South Beach Casa Nora Hotel*. It isn't long after departing the scene that his phone rings. Once again it's his boss.

"We are down to the last man. They say he's invincible. Whatever you do I want him alive. This is like your Holy grail"

"Let me call you back,"

Says Rude Buay.

Rude Buay ponders the statement. In his mind, he knows Alberto Gomez's life has been spared many times, at his own hands. He knows what he has lived through at the hands of the most notorious Drug Czar to ever run a cartel, Gomez. Chelo sitting in the passenger seat senses Rude Buay's confusion.

Rude Buay calls back Ortiz.

"Sorry boss, no can do. When I catch Alberto Gomez I am going to kill him. Whether that pleases you or not, this man has been a menace to society. He has caused many innocent kids to die by his actions. It's like asking me to spare a thousand *Osamas*. Do you know what we are in for if he continues to breathe any longer."

Ortiz on the other end of the phone is not giving up and persists in his demands to Rude Buay.

"Just bring him in, Agent Bascombe."

"I am sorry you will have to come and get him yourself if you want him under those conditions."

Rude Buay puts Ortiz on speakerphone. He radios the rest of his agents:

"When we catch up to Albert Gomez, no matter what's the condition let me have him. I want to be the one to drill his skull."

Rude Buay hangs up the call with his boss and pulls up outside the hotel.

He speaks to the manager sitting behind the desk. The MOD is a middle-aged woman of Cuban descent. The woman focuses more on Chelo than on Rude Buay.

"I am looking for Alberto Gomez," says Rude Buay disclosing his badge.

"No."

Responds the woman nervously.

"That's okay. There is no need to be afraid of him. Gomez can't harm you."

Says Chelo.

"You all got to be crazy,"

Responds the woman.

"We are not. We just need to talk to him,"

Says Rude Buay.

He reaches inside his pocket, pulls out a money clip and peels off 5 one hundred dollar bills. The woman's eyes light up.

"Executive floor on the 23rd floor but I forgot he has tight security. Do you want your money back?"

"That's okay keep it."

Say Rude Buay.

He leaves in haste to his car and picks up his *Fast and Furious* ammunition; Chelo also arms himself as well. The other agents are also armed and ready.

The MOD is alarmed as Baptiste is stationed in the parking lot, Mildred is in the lobby, Hudson heads for the elevator, Chelo takes the stairwell. Banks takes the stairs to the 23rd floor covering Rude Buay. Upon arriving, Rude Buay and Banks see the two guards pacing the 23rd floor. Rude Buay pops one while Banks pops the other.

Rude Buay knocks on the door to Gomez's suite. There is no answer. Although they can hear the TV playing no one answers the door. Rude Buay kicks in the door. On the table in the room, there are used freebasing utensils along with Alberto Gomez's *F & F* gun. Rude Buay grabs the gun and charges in with both guns; his and Gomez's

Alberto Gomez dashes out of the bathroom wearing a white bathrobe. He launches for his weapon on the table. Rude Buay shows it to him while balancing his on the other hand.

"Those guards just lost their jobs."

Rude Buay senses that Gomez is trying to make small talk so he could arm himself or buy time. Gomez looks peripherally for a substitute weapon. At this point, even a table knife would do in Gomez's mind. Just some kind of defense but there is none.

"I don't think you have the balls to shoot me Rude Buay."

"How about a fingernail every day for the next ten days?"

Asks Rude Buay,

Banks edges closer.

"Or how about both your eyes right now?"

"FYI, I am here to torture you before the vultures have you for their delight."

Says Rude Buay.

"So you are into Moses' law."

Banks is animated and ready to end Gomez's life.

"*An eye for an eye or a tooth for a tooth*? I thought you were all about the Messiah. Who said, *Forgive and it shall be forgiven you*."

Continues Gomez.

"There is nothing to talk about. Let's shoot the bastard!"

Says Walter Banks,

Rude Buay shoots Gomez in the right leg with his gun and blows it off. The residue of that round leaves a huge hole in the wall.

"I am trying to be like the Messiah, It's a tough job. He walked on water, didn't he? Then he turned water into wine. He even healed the sick. He also made the lame man walk."

Says Rude Buay.

"Shoot the sucker; don't let him break you down,"

Says Banks.

Rude Buay shoots Gomez in the other leg, this time with the Drug Czars' gun. Gomez is now on the floor, both legs severed from the knees down. He is undergoing tremendous pain.

"Jesus also knelt and prayed, didn't he?"

Says Rude Buay.

Alberto Gomez is groaning and in pain.

Rude Buay looks at Gomez's two jumping legs while the Czar continues to suffer.

"Cuff him Banks!"

Banks lays his weapon on the table and place handcuffs on the bleeding Alberto Gomez.

Rude Buay takes out his cell phone and dials his boss Ortiz.

"We've got him. He is now yours. FYI, he is going to need a pair of crutches."

"Great job! I'll get some to him soon."

Says Ortiz.

Rude Buay and Banks exit the room and team up with the other agents in the parking lot. *They drive to D.E.A. Headquarters.*

About The Author

John A. Andrews, screenwriter, producer, and author of several books, founded Teen Success in 2009. Its mission statement: ***To empower Teens in maximizing their full potential to be successful and contributing citizens in the world.*** As an author of books on relationships, personal development, and vivid engaging stories, John is sought after as a motivational speaker to address success principles to young adults. John makes an impact in the lives of others because of his passion and commitment to make a difference in the world. Being a father of three sons propels John even more in his desire to see teens succeed. Andrews, a divorced dad of three sons ages 17, 15 and 13, was born in the Islands of St. Vincent and the Grenadines. He grew up in a home of five sisters and three brothers. He recounts: "My parents were all about values: work hard, love God and never give up on your dreams."

Self educated, John developed an interest for music. Although lacking the formal education, he later put his knowledge and passion to good use, moonlighting as a disc jockey in New York. This paved the way for further exploration in the world of entertainment. In 1994 John caught the acting bug. Leaving the Big Apple for Hollywood over a decade ago not only put several national TV commercials under his belt but helped him to find his niche.

His passion for writing started in 2002, when he was denied the rights to a 1970's classic film, which he so badly wanted to remake. In 2007, while etching two of his original screenplays, he published his first book "The 5 Steps to Changing Your Life" Currently he's publishing a string of novels, coaching two of his sons who are writing their first novel, bringing some of his work to the big screen, while working on empowering teens worldwide.

In 2008 he not only published his second book but also wrote seven additional books that year, and produced the docu-drama based on his second book; *Spread Some Love (Relationships 101)*.

See Imdb: http://www.imdb.com/title/tt0854677/.

FOR MORE ON
BOOKS THAT WILL ENHANCE YOUR LIFE ™
Visit: **A L I**
www.AndrewsLeadershipInternational.com
EMAIL US
john@johnaandrews.com

Website
www.JohnAAndrews.com

*Rude Buay is a drug prevention chronicle about teens caught up in the war on drugs and contains content for adults; parental discretion is advised for children.

Resource:
Methamphetamine:
http://www.nmtf.us/methamphetamine/metha
phetamine.htm

News Report: ABC News

THE MACOS ADVENTURE

RENEGADE COPS

CROSS ATLANTIC FIASCO

BLOOD IS THICKER THAN WATER

JOHN A. ANDREWS

RENEGADE COPS

Creator of

The RUDE BUAY Series

&

The WHODUNIT CHRONICLES

WHO SHOT THE SHERRIFF?

RUDE BUAY ... THE
UNSTOPPABLE

CHICO RUDO

CHICO RUDO II

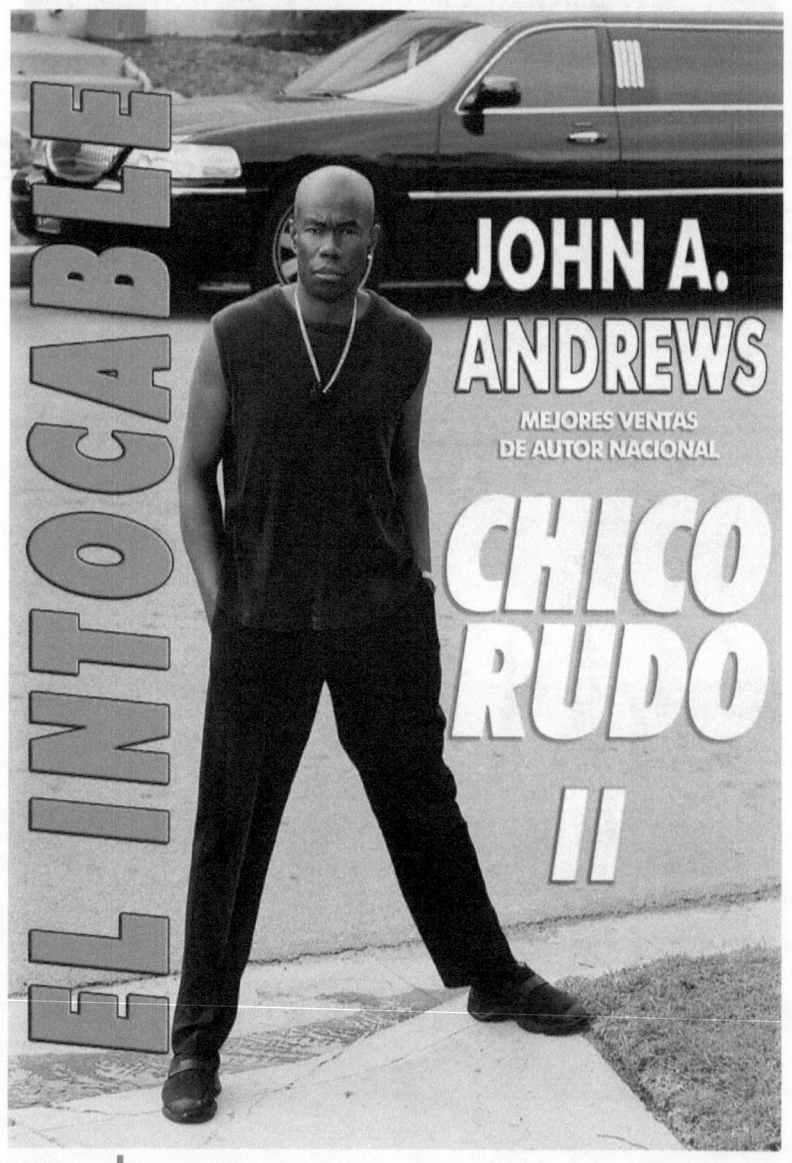

AUTHOR OF THE RUDE BUAY SERIES
JOHN A. ANDREWS
A MEMOIR IN TWO VOLUMES

HOW I RAISED MYSELF

FROM FAILURE TO SUCCESS

IN HOLLYWOOD

QUOTES UNLIMITED II

ANDREWS

"QUOTES"

UNLIMITED
Vol. II

Over 400 Quotes From Over 18 Books!

John A. Andrews

National Bestselling Author of

RUDE BUAY ... THE UNSTOPPABLE

NATIONAL BESTSELLING AUTHOR
John A. Andrews

spread
some
LOVE
Relationships 101
REVISED EDITION

National Bestselling Author of
Rude Buay ... The Unstoppable

THE 5 STEPS TO CHANGING YOUR LIFE

BY: JOHN A. ANDREWS

WHEN THE DUST SETTLES

I AM STILL STANDING

A TRUE HOLLYWOOD STORY

starring

John A. Andrews

NATIONAL BESTSELLING AUTHOR OF RUDE BUAY ... THE UNSTOPPABLE

DARE TO MAKE A DIFFERENCE

SUCCESS 101

FOR

ADULTS

#1 INTERNATIONAL BESTSELLING AUTHOR

JOHN A. ANDREWS

By National Bestselling Author of Rude Buay ... The Unstoppable

TOTAL COMMITMENT

The Mindset of Champions

JOHN A. ANDREWS

AUTHOR OF NATIONAL BestSeller *RUDE BUAY ... THE UNSTOPPABLE*

Whose Woman Was She?

A TRUE
HOLLYWOOD
STORY...

John A. Andrews

NATIONAL BESTSELLING AUTHOR
John A. Andrews

spread
some
LOVE
Relationships 101
REVISED EDITION

VISIT: WWW.JOHNAANDREWS.COM